REA

...**The Black Elvis**

Jackie Wilson...

Doug Carter

...The Black Elvis

Jackie Wilson...

Doug Carter

Jacksonville, Florida

FIRST EDITION
Book design by Greg Molloy, MacMedia Graphics
Printed by: Rose Printing Company, Inc.
Manufactured in the United States of America.

Photographs courtesy of Doug Carter's private collection, front cover from the
Brunswick LP "Jackie Sings the Blues," back cover photos from Brunswick
LP's "He's So Fine," "Soul Galore" and "Baby Workout." Spotlight on Jackie
Wilson series: Ray Flerlage/Michael Ochs Archives/Venice, CA.

Photo of Jackie Wilson and LaVern Baker, BMI Photo Archive/Michael Ochs
Archives/Venice, CA.

Photo from the movie: "Go, Johnny, Go" and the studio publicity photo from
Super Stock 7660, Centurion Parkway, Jacksonville, Florida 32256

(904) 565-0066

Billboard Trade Ads courtesy of Showtime Archives (Toronto)

Photo of Jackie Wilson with Nat Tarnopol and Alan Freed, from the Gordon
Anderson Collection, Schomburg Center for Research in Black Culture, 515
Malcom X Boulevard, New York, New York 10037

Jackie leaving hospital with wife and mother UPI/Corbis-Bettman.

"The Album Covers" from Brunswick Records

Dedication

This book is dedicated to my parents. My father, William G. Ellsworth, Jr., who passed away in March of 1996, taught me that love has nothing to do with the color of skin. Ahead of his time in the appreciation of music, my father thoroughly enjoyed and respected the talents of any race or nationality and gladly took me to see several Jackie Wilson shows at times and places where whites were rarely seen. I am grateful to my mother, Hope L. Ellsworth, for her support and loving tolerance for my obsession with this story.

Foreword

Anyone old enough to remember the horrible news that President John F. Kennedy had been shot recalls where he or she was and what he or she was doing at that exact moment. The event created a shock wave and collective societal trauma that would become a powerful factor in our shared American experience. That night, November 22, 1963, Jackie Wilson, known in the music world as "Mr. Excitement," was scheduled to perform at the Memorial Coliseum in Jacksonville, Florida, my hometown at the time. Other performers that night included Cassius Clay (now Muhammad Ali), Redd Foxx, and Chuck Jackson. Most people went home that night and glued themselves to a television to witness the assassination, hoping to learn why this tragic deed had occurred, robbing them of their beloved leader and friend. My father had already paid for tickets to take me to the concert, so we decided to attend as planned. Still in a state of semi-shock, we witnessed a performance that, for its duration, not only overshadowed our terrible sadness but became a pivotal experience in my life.

Due to the events of the day, the crowd at the Coliseum started out subdued. Yet by the time Mr. Excitement stepped out from behind the curtain, took a puff from a cigarette, dropped it, then ground it out with the toe of his black wingtip shoe, they were like a school of frenzied fish. Jackie ran to center stage where "Gorgeous" George, the emcee of the show, spun around, tossing the microphone high into the air. Jackie spun around, caught the microphone, adjusted his powder blue jacket, and began to prove himself to be the greatest rock and roll showman of all time, a man Elvis Presley himself called the "Black Elvis."

Elvis and Jackie had a great deal in common. Both were rock and roll pioneers—each a favorite artist of the other. Their lives and careers ran virtually parallel in time, yet there were distinctive, telling opposites—one was black, one white; one from the urban north, the other from the rural south; the yin and the yang.

Jackie, born just seven months before Elvis in a Detroit, Michigan, ghetto, came from gospel music roots. Elvis, born in Tupelo, Mississippi, also sprang from poor beginnings and sang church music in his youth. Both men lived hard lives in the fast lane of the music world. Their careers ended tragically, similarly and not far apart in time. At age forty-one Jackie suffered what was thought to be a massive heart attack while performing on stage in Cherry Hill, New Jersey. He fell into a coma from which he awoke four months later but was left incapacitated and totally dependent, physically, emotionally, and financially ruined for the remainder of his life. Elvis would come to Jackie's rescue and contribute money for his convalescent care, only to die himself not long afterward at age forty-two from heart failure. Neither of these extremely talented men left estates anywhere commensurate with their lifetime earnings.

During the time-span of their careers, a whole era of music history took place, too much of which has been forgotten, unrecognized and unrewarded by the American music public. Among the larger oversights are the contributions of Jackie Wilson.

The continual circular influence of these two stars began early in Jackie's career. His very first hit *Reet Petite* in 1957 was called "Elvis pastiche" by one critic; another critic called it a "blaring up tempo novelty song that featured Wilson mimicking Elvis Presley's stuttering, breathless vocal delivery." *Reet Petite* was only one of Jackie's fifty-four singles that would make Billboard's weekly record charts, more than any other black artist of his time. Upon release in England thirty years later, three years after Jackie's death, *Reet Petite* went to the top of the British charts for five weeks during Christmas, selling more than 800,000 copies, and generating a popular video.

It is common knowledge in the recording industry that it is much easier to cheat someone out of money due them from record royalties and live performances than from movie deals. Jackie never made it to the movies because his career was guided solely by the greed of his management, Brunswick Records. Jackie recorded the songs Brunswick wanted him to sing, performed where he was told to perform, and molded his style at the direction of his manager, Nat Tarnopol. Mismanagement could not hide his talent, but it did not make the most of it, and consequently Jackie Wilson died a poor, destitute invalid while lawsuits and countersuits swirled about him without his knowledge.

Brunswick had a dynamo by the tail. Jackie Wilson exuded tremendous energy and stamina. If I were limited to one word to describe the difference between Jackie and all other performers of his kind, I would choose the word "bounce," a trait most likely the result of his early years as a boxer. In an interview with radio personality Norman Knight, he asked Jackie, "What makes Jackie Wilson go?"

Jackie responded, "There's somewhere I want to go. I just don't know where. I want to act, but not necessarily. Secretly I want to be a disc jockey. "

Norm then asked, "If you could be a disc jockey for one hour and I put you in a studio to play records and I gave you a stack of one kind of music or one type of performer, who would you play?"

Without hesitation, Jackie replied, "Elvis Presley, 'cause he's a good friend of mine, and I know a lot about him. I could talk a lot about him, and I mean in a very nice way. Well, he also did me a great favor once. I was in Hollywood, California, and I was playing a club called "The Trip," and we had a little difficulty getting people to come out at that particular time. So he came out twice for me. Well, you couldn't get in! People said 'Hey, if Elvis goes, then let us go, man.'"

Because of misguided management and the color barriers of the times, Jackie never became the international star he deserved to be. The color barriers sometimes were invisible. Few blacks got speaking roles in Hollywood, much less starring roles, but I believe

Jackie's performing ability would have allowed him to transcend the times and break those barriers. He did it with his music, and he would have done it in the film medium as well. Jackie was a movie star who never made a movie.

When Elvis appeared at the Florida Theater in Jacksonville in August 1956, it became front page news as a result of a warning issued by juvenile court judge Marion Gooding that Elvis keep his act clean of bumps and grinds or face court charges. Judge Gooding even attended the performance himself to make sure his orders were obeyed. However, when Jackie Wilson headlined the show in the Coliseum (1963), a building that drew thousands more people, the two major papers in town made no mention of it either before or after the performance. Nonetheless, word spread within the black community and more than 6,000 people packed the auditorium. My father and I were one of the few white faces in the crowd. "You can feel the electricity," my father said to me.

Jackie was the purest vocalist of his generation, the most hypnotic performer ever. His vocal range was incredible; his physical stamina was phenomenal. He was a veritable acrobat. He executed leaps, jumps, splits, dropping to his knees with the microphone, then moved into shimmies, twists, one-legged sidesteps, boxing moves, and 360-degree spins. He was never out of breath, though he collapsed to the stage pleading for love from the frenzied females in the front rows. From the moment he burst through the curtain, even before he sang one note, the crowd was hysterical. Before long, Jackie removed his jacket and twirled it above his head, teasing the crazed females even further, then threw it into the audience where it disappeared like meat in pool of piranha. His tie met the same fate, and Jackie never missed a note.

During a slow song he lay on the edge of the stage with body-guards on each side allowing the wild, out-of-control female fans to mob, grab, and maul him. His body dropped out of sight; his voice was the only evidence he was still alive. When he reappeared, he was drenched in perspiration, his processed hair askew, and his shirt torn to shreds exposing a scar from a gunshot wound. A wink told his fans he was happy to be there, while the smile on his face radiated sexual power.

Judge Gooding would have split a gut.

That seminal night in 1963 remained forever imprinted in my consciousness and would influence my life in tangible ways. Odell "Gorgeous" George was a show himself that night, decked out in a different suit each time he appeared on stage to introduce another performer. He dazzled the audience and worked them up by having them spell out in an ever-rising crescendo:

J - A - C - K - I - E   W - I - L - S - O - N.

When Jackie appeared from behind the curtain, Gorgeous George did a 360-degree spin, tossed the microphone in the air for Jackie to snatch in his own 360.

In a recording studio in Atlanta, Georgia, in 1990, I ran into Gorgeous George working on some new music. He was "Gracious" George with me and spent a great deal of time talking with me about Jackie Wilson and sharing his intimate knowledge of the star and the man. For instance, George recollected that it was fortunate Jackie loved to fight and was good at it. Occasionally, men would wait outside his stage door and because of the way Jackie danced and crooned his love songs, they would call him a sissy and egg him into fights. Jackie would tear into them with all the boxing prowess he learned in his early days in the ring in Detroit.

Gorgeous George emceed for virtually all the rhythm and blues stars of the day. I asked him who he thought was the greatest performer he had ever seen, and his answer confirmed what I always felt: without hesitating a two-count, George said, "Jackie Wilson."

George recalled how Jackie and Sam Cooke would take turns headlining shows, but that Sam, a handsome and talented star in his own right, was always concerned when he followed Jackie because evidently Jackie would work the women into such a state of passion that Sam feared he would be nothing more than a letdown. George told Sam his secret: *drop to your knees during the performance*. It worked like a charm!

Many years after seeing Jackie perform, I was doing stand-up comedy at the Punch Line Comedy Club in Atlanta, Georgia. While not doing what you'd call a full-fledged impersonation of Jackie, I did adopt some of his stylistic techniques to test the effect they would have on my audience. Since I don't smoke, I substituted a rolled paper for a cigarette, ground it into the stage floor, grabbed the microphone and called out, "Man, I feel GOOD! Just quit smoking!" When I saw that worked, I threw my tie into the crowd. Darned if that didn't work, too. No wonder everyone copied Jackie.

I eventually gave up comedy but I had learned showmanship from a master. For my money, the only way to top a Jackie Wilson performance was to leap into the air and fly. Rhythm and blues singer Etta James was right on target when she said of Jackie, "He was surely the greatest showman of his day, a great singer and acrobatic dancer who did for soul-stepping what Michael Jordan did for basketball—took it to a higher level."

Perhaps the death of President John F. Kennedy made me overly susceptible to any outside influence on that particular night of my life—the night I saw Jackie Wilson perform at the Coliseum in Jacksonville, Florida. Nonetheless, it was as if my psyche lay like an open wound and anything that happened by would have filled it up. But Jackie Wilson's performance moved something deep inside me that has never waned. It awakened in me the love of song and the appreciation of inborn musical talent perfected by a lifetime of dedicated effort. I was only seventeen years old, but I was suddenly old enough to know that entertainment would be my life. The memory of that night and the decision I made propelled me in front of a radio station microphone as a deejay for many years to come. I was a dedicated Jackie Wilson fan and spun his records for all my listeners.

Since 1975 I have collected newspaper and magazine articles written about Jackie throughout his career and talked with various individuals who were a part of Jackie's life and who shared their experiences and insights with me. I have used the words of these interviewees and writers of the times liberally because they were first-hand observers and told their stories better than I could. I am indebted to all those people who gave their time and shared their intimate memories with me.

I think of Jackie's career as starting with a bang, ending with a bang, and having a bang in the middle. That his life should end with a whimper is a tragedy every bit as monumental as his influence on the world of modern music. I have written this book in the hope that people too young or too unlucky to have seen him perform would be able to experience a small part of a most remarkable man and understand the impact he had on the course of music history. Jackie Wilson marked me in an indelible way, as he did so many others who appreciated his talent as an entertainer and his generosity and compassion as a man. This book, a lifetime labor of love, is the payment of my debt to him and a tribute to his memory.

—*DOUG CARTER*

JACKSONVILLE, FLORIDA, 1998

Acknowledgments

Bobby Bland, Bill Brant, G.C. Cameron, Reverend Anthony Campbell, Marian Cocke, Geraldine Collins, Bill Frazier, Odell 'Gorgeous' George, Mildred Graham, Betty Gordon, Frank Green, Lynn Guidry, Kim Harper, Steve Hayes, Richard Johnson, Selvia Landin, Greg Molloy, Debra Moss, John Mulkerin, Bill Murry, Lots a' Poppa, Joseph Redding, Tom Saitta, August Sims, Percy Sledge, Toni Lynn Washington, George West, Jerry West, Ken Williams, Lawrence Williams, Harlean Wilson.

This book would not have been possible without the writing skills of Debra Baukney Moss, who took my years of research — gathered from every imaginable source and form — and helped to create a fascinating story long overdue to the American public.

Table of Contents

...The Black Elvis
Jackie Wilson...

Chapter One

The First Bang
Rags to Riches

Some people in the crowd were screaming the countdown along with the announcer over the loud speaker and referee in the ring: "Ten! Nine! Eight! . . . Jack "Sonny" Wilson lay face down on the edge of the mat. He had taken a hard left hook under the eye, and it was starting to swell and throb. Dazed, his one good eye scanned the crowd for his mother. She had been there a second ago in the third row, as he had heard her call, "Sonny!" Nevertheless, the Detroit boxing arena was pandemonium, and the noise was drowned out by the numbness in his face. It would soon be over, he thought. This would turn out to be true, not only for this bout, but for the rest of his boxing career. Jack Wilson was destined for bigger things, a world of wilder crowds and longer, more painful bouts with drugs, alcohol and fame—the world of entertainment.

Little is known of Jack Leroy Wilson's early life growing up in

Detroit in the 1930s and 40s. Most of what has been written starts with his winning the American Golden Gloves welterweight title as a teenager. Some of his biographers say he gained entry to the prestigious boxing title fights by lying about his age. Others assert the whole Golden Gloves issue was a marketing ploy instituted by Brunswick Records to boost his appeal.

Fact or fiction, Jackie Wilson apparently believed he had been a Golden Gloves contender. In one of the few surviving examples of his own words, he told Norman Knight in an interview: "I actually did not want to leave [boxing]. My mother just grabbed me by the hair one day and told me, 'no more.' Well, actually, what happened— I had a good record, and I had won Golden Gloves in Michigan with a mustache and the whole bit. I was only about sixteen and you're supposed to be eighteen. I was just getting real good and she walked into the arena one night and I was boxing. I always looked for her in a certain seat and she wasn't there and all of a sudden she walked in. My nickname is Sonny. She hollers out really loud, 'Hey, Sonny, Hey Sonny,' and I turned around. Wop, wop, wop. So she finally saw me get beat to bits, so she told me no more."

Some of what is known from Jackie's early years comes from a man he grew up with named Dr. Anthony Campbell. Reverend Campbell is the current pastor of the Russell Street Baptist Church in Detroit and the son of the man who was the pastor of the same congregation when Jackie's mother, grandmother and siblings attended during Jackie's formative years.

According to Reverend Campbell, Jackie's mother, Eliza Mae (nee Ranson), was a decent, hardworking, God-fearing woman. Raised in Columbus, Mississippi, she moved north to work in a Dodge automobile factory. After World War II, when most of the black women were laid off, she took in foster children and earned income caring for them. This was considered a very honorable profession then, and many of those children, who would otherwise have remained in an orphanage, were given a chance to live in a home with a family. Eliza Mae lost two children before Jackie's birth in June 1934. This fact may have contributed to her desire to have more children around her and her propensity for doting on Jackie.

Jackie's father, Jack, was a chronic alcoholic and was out of work most of the time. As to any influence he may have had during Jackie's formative years, by the age of six, Jackie and his father were singing together on street corners for money. By age nine Jackie, too, was using the money they made to buy wine.

Also according to Campbell, he and Jackie lived in a neighborhood that would produce many famous entertainers. "Four blocks from my house lived Aretha Franklin and right behind me on Belmont Street was Smokey Robinson. We were in kindergarten together, Smokey and I. And Aretha's father was a preacher and my father was a preacher. Jackie was a north-end kid, which was where affluent and upwardly mobile blacks moved in the forties, and that is where I met him.

"In school, Jackie was a class clown, always entertaining. And he would sing louder in the choir than anybody else. You know, if he'd see a group he liked or admired [he would imitate them]. Then he could imitate the Ink Spots; he could imitate Nat King Cole. You have to realize that without television, CDs, and boom boxes, we entertained ourselves with our voices. You didn't carry a radio on the front porch. You would simply imitate the songs that you heard."

Some biographers have written that Jackie got his street smarts and fighting ability in gangs, specifically a group called The Shakers. Others claim his truancy resulted in a temporary incarceration in Lansing Correctional Institute and that he learned to box there. In his book, **Smokey: Inside My Life,** Smokey Robinson, lead singer of the Miracles and vice president of Motown Records, writes about the first time he saw Jackie Wilson: "I was raised when the quality of street music was extremely high. There was no screaming, no faking, and no farting around. If you couldn't sing, forget it, but if you could, women were yours.

"I remember once looking out the window and seeing this long limo arriving on our block.

"Who is it? I asked myself, thinking it had to be the mayor or governor. Turned out to be someone even more important—Jackie Wilson.

"Jackie was a local hero, the cat who took Clyde McPhatter's place with the Dominoes. He had been a leader of the Shakers, one of Detroit's most notorious gangs. He'd also been a Golden Gloves boxer. He could sing high, low and ever' which way; with his smooth moves and natural polish, he could out-dance Fred Astaire. He was rugged, handsome, had processed hair, and big flashy eyes. When I saw him that day on our street visiting his cousins, it was like seeing some god.

"See, in my neighborhood, we idolized the entertainers, the preachers, and the pimps. They were the ones with the sharp clothes, the Cadillac cars, and the fine women. They had the glory."

As to Jackie's involvement in gangs and the implicit suggestion of violence or crime that association entailed, Reverend Campbell feels gangs as we know them today were quite different when Jackie was involved with them.

"Everybody was a member of the Shakers. There were the Shakers, the Seven Crowns. Gangs then were not like gangs now. Gangs now are drug and criminal syndicates. Gangs then represented turf and territorial issues and the Shakers were kind of the north-end gang. They would have a turf from the river out to say Six or Seven Mile Road, to between Highland Park on the west side and Hamtramick, which was Polish on the east side. So, that's like saying he was a member of the boys' athletic club. I mean, everybody belonged to the Shakers or the Seven Crowns.

"I think it is pretentious to say that [Jackie was a gang leader] and probably represents more of an appetite for self-aggrandizement on his part or others. He was not a gang leader. He was not criminally involved. Now, he's always been a leader because he was the class clown and he could sing and he was good looking. But I would not say under any reasonable stretch of the imagination that he was a gang leader."

Taking the few accounts of Jackie's so-called gang life into consideration, the more likely explanation is that Jackie was more of a status symbol for the Shakers than an actual participating member. Some accounts suggest that in recompense for the status his name afforded them, they protected him when he sang in some of the more dangerous Detroit neighborhoods.

About his quitting boxing, however, Reverend Campbell confirmed most accounts that Mrs. Wilson was the one who threw in Jackie's towel. Campbell recalls, "She did not approve of his boxing and did not think it was a legitimate way to make a living and she always protested it. My father always protested it. Of course, boxing then was controlled by gangsters. So to be a boxer meant that you were cavorting with gangsters."

Other insights into Jackie's early boxing career came from his first association with Berry Gordy, Jr., who would go on to write some of Jackie's first hit records and later become the founder and president of Motown Records. Jackie was a few years younger than Gordy, but both grew up in the ghettos of Detroit and learned to defend themselves to survive. That they may have actually boxed each other is speculation, but they undoubtedly associated in the same clubs.

Etta James, one of the greatest rhythm and blues and soul singers of all time, was a friend of Jackie's for many years. In her autobiography entitled **The Etta James Story: Rage to Survive**, James promulgated the Golden Gloves misconception and recalled a time during 1962 when Jackie called upon his boxing talents during an altercation in which Jackie "whaled away" on Etta's then-boyfriend. She called Jackie's hands "lethal weapons."

The hype is further inflamed by Ralph M. Newman and Alan Kaltman in the *Time Barrier Express* article "Lonely Teardrops— The Story of a Forgotten Man." They claimed, "Jackie entered the ring at age 11 or 12, eventually winning the Detroit Golden Gloves in 1950. No sooner did he seem destined for a pro career than his mother put her foot down.

"'Nobody was gonna mess up my pretty boy's face,' she's reputed to have said, a philosophy not entirely alien to Jackie himself. And so, the fighting career became history just as quickly as it began, but not without affecting his outlook on life."

In penning the liner notes for Rhino Records' boxed set of Jackie Wilson's recordings, Robert Pruter compiled one of the most thorough biographies of Wilson ever done. Pruter, R&B editor of **Goldmine** and author of the book **Chicago Soul**, relied heavily on interviews with Dick Jacobs, Henry Jerome, Roquel Davis, Billy Davis, Carl Davis, Simon Rutberg and Steve Towne, all people intimately familiar with Jackie Wilson's life. It is from Billy Davis that he learned the truth behind the Golden Gloves lie: "One of his [Jackie's] early enthusiasms was boxing, but contrary to most published reports on Wilson's career he never won the Detroit Golden Gloves and most certainly never fought professionally. Detroit guitarist Billy Davis, who knew Wilson since he was fourteen years old related, 'After Jackie got a little fame with *Lonely Teardrops* and all that, the record company built up his biography. He was never any kind of champion; he was just a tough street kid who fought a few bouts in the clubs, like Brewster Center and the CYP Center.'

"Davis was a gym rat and hung around all the boxing clubs in Detroit and was thoroughly familiar with the scene, so believe him when he says Wilson was never a Golden Gloves champ or a professional."

What we do know is that Jackie lived in a place called Corner Garden on Detroit's north side and attended Highland Park High School, which according to Reverend Campbell was a predominantly white school, first generation Polish and Jewish for the most part. Highland Park offered a better education than the public schools serving the neighborhood where Jackie lived. Despite his interest in boxing, Jackie had no other known sport interests. "I didn't know Jackie to have any other hobbies either," recalls Campbell. "Other than women and music. Was he popular with the girls? Oh, that's putting it mildly!"

Jackie's attitude and relationships with women were formed during this period of his life. "Jackie had a reputation for being abusive toward his women in the sense that they would fight each other; they would pitch battles." Campbell said. "It wasn't like what under modern pander would be called abusive relationships, it was simply [a] *tit for tat* kind of thing."

Jackie was ten years old when he met Freda Hood, the woman who would become his first wife. She became pregnant by Jackie at age seventeen, and they were married in a small wedding in her home. Sometime during this period Eliza Mae and Jack, Sr., separated and Jackie's mother began living with a man named Johnny Lee. Jackie dropped out of school in the ninth grade and began working in the Ford foundry. The job lasted only a few weeks. Jackie told his mother the work hurt his hands.

Eliza Mae was always a strong influence on her son. Emcee Bill Murry met Jackie when Jackie was around nineteen and got to know his mother. "His mom was dangerous, boy. She could con the huns off a billygoat. And she did all that stuff for the children, you know. She was a fast talker, charismatic, everybody liked her, but she knew how to work the system for the shortcomings that they lacked, what the family lacked in money. And, Jackie was her baby." After leaving school, Jackie held various jobs but had little appetite for standard employment and never stayed at one job too long. With the apparent blessing of his mother, Jackie began singing with church groups and in local clubs. According to Jackie his mother sang but he didn't like instruments and never studied music. He also said in an interview once that he enjoyed singing spirituals and gospel in Mother Bradley's Church because it gave him good feelings.

Race music, as it was called then, was evolving, and with the Ever Ready Gospel Singers Jackie would develop the more soulful qualities of his multifaceted repertoire. Black Detroit was a hotbed of budding music artists and many of Jackie's early gig partners, such as Levi Stubbs, who would later sing with the Four Tops, made names for themselves as well. Jackie hooked up with the Thrillers, whose members Sonny Woods and Hank Ballard would later form the Royals and evolve into Hank Ballard and the Midnighters. Jackie also formed a group called the Falcons (not to be confused with the group formed later by Wilson Pickett).

Although Elvis Presley was still in high school in 1951 and other than hanging out at Memphis blues joints and gospel "sings," he had taken no formal steps to launch his singing career. 1951 was the beginning for Jackie. His first break came in a recording debut with two singles for Dizzy Gillespie's Dee Gee label, the first of his many versions of *Danny Boy* and *Rainy Day Blues.* On the flip sides were *Rockaway Rock* and *Bulldozer Blues*, which were released in 1952. 1951 was also the year Jackie appeared at Detroit's Paradise Theater where Johnny Otis hosted a talent contest.

At that time there was a group of black vaudeville theaters called "Around the World" theaters — the Apollo, the Howard, the Regal, the Royal, and the Paradise in Detroit were all part of this group. Whenever Johnny Otis was touring with his band, The Johnny Otis Show, he would try to persuade the owner to host a talent contest in an effort to spot new, emerging talent. The manager of the Paradise was more than accommodating, allowing the one-hour contest to stretch to an hour and a half. Still, only half the kids wanting to perform did so, while the rest waited in the wings.

In Arnold Shaw's comprehensive book **Honkers and Shouters- The Golden Years of Rhythm and Blues**, Johnny Otis told his version of the first time he heard Jackie sing. "I was serving as a talent scout for King Records," Otis writes. "When I phoned Syd Nathan in Cincinnati, he quickly agreed to send somebody to Detroit. That night, as we waited, I wrote a song for Jackie, who seemed to need material. It was called *Every Beat of My Heart*. Jackie learned it and sang it for the producer Nathan sent, but he preferred the vocal group, probably because King was doing great with Billy Ward and The Dominoes. King was vocal group conscious. He kinda ignored Little Willie John and Jackie Wilson—and poor Jackie, who sang in a very high tenor, really sang his heart out. But he took the song with him and recorded it with The Royals [later known as the Midnighters]. . . In later years, when I thought of what Berry Gordy did in Detroit, I was not surprised. For some reason, Detroit was loaded with talent; it just needed the vision and the creative power of Gordy to help it mature. A tremendous percentage of the young people heard at the Paradise were talented. Three of them made a strong impression. They were Little Willie John, Jackie Wilson, and the Royals, featuring Hank Ballard.

Johnny Otis later became known as the Godfather of rhythm and blues, though he was not black, because of his success as a talent scout. He was born of Greek parents and raised in an integrated neighborhood in Berkeley, California. While a teenager he adopted black culture, wed a black woman, and remained in the ghetto for the rest of his life. Otis played drums with several well-known black groups, including Louis Jordan's, and in 1948 opened a rhythm and blues nightclub called the Barrelhouse Club. Otis is credited with discovering many black artists like T-Bone Walker,

Little Willie John, Hank Ballard, Little Esther Phillips, The Robins, Etta James, and Jackie Wilson. Some believe Billy Ward deserves more credit for discovering Jackie Wilson.

Jackie claims to have won Otis' contests often, but the one he did not win would be the most important to his career. As Jackie tells it: "Once Johnny Otis was there and heard me, around 1951. He got in touch with Syd Nathan, King Records. Syd sent Ralph Bass. He heard me. He heard Little Willie John. He heard The Dominoes. He passed me and Willie John, signed the Dominoes. But Billy Ward, who ran The Dominoes, took my name and number. I went to work at Lee's Sensation Club. Must have been seventeen."

Although Jackie did not win that particular contest, and Ward would not call him for another year, Jackie's fresh talent and raw energy never left his mind.

"After a year, Billy Ward phoned me, "Jackie once recalled. "[I] was sure he never remembered me, but there he was on the phone. So I became part of The Dominoes in 1953. Clyde McPhatter was lead singer. I also sang lead." Jackie began touring with the Dominoes in April of that year. Ironically, Elvis Presley, still in high school, entered his first talent contest at Humes High and received rave reviews from the audience.

Reverend Campbell was a big Jackie Wilson fan by this time and saw him perform many times during this period. "There was kind of an amateur night phenomena... at a black vaudeville spot called Paradise. Now there were two basic black vaudeville places in the city. There was one called the Paradise and the other one was… it became the Broadway, I can't remember its original name. But at black vaudeville, you would go for a matinee on Saturday and you would see the Step Brothers or the Nicholas Brothers or Pinkney Markham and they always had an amateur feature. And then as now to some extent, you went to the amateur circuit to get a presence in front of audiences and to be seen by agents or hustlers or record producers and what not. So, 1 saw Jackie in about a dozen amateur shows at high schools. At places like the Paradise and at others. There was a group in my father's church called the Dynamos, so I would slur the name. I would say, 'I'm going to go see the Dynamos tonight.' 'Oh yeah, good, go ahead.' I end up at the Paradise, which is now Orchestra Hall here, listening to him jam. When he started doing club dates, you had to be able to buy a drink or something. I couldn't go when he did club dates. So, in the black vaudeville circuit, I saw him starting out."

There are no known tapes of Jackie's performances from this time so again we are left with Reverend Campbell's recollections of Jackie's style as he was still developing it. The early groin exhibitionism that Michael Jackson made his own was shocking audiences in the 1950s, but it was fascinating them at the same time. "The fancy footwork was not something unique with him. What was unique about Jackie was his incredible energy and his ability to dramatize. I mean, it literally set a style… when you did a romantic ballad you pleaded with the women in the audience and you opened up your shirt. If you were doing something that was sexual in nature, you were very explicit about the use of your groin, falling on the floor and all of that. [Jackie] was athletic. He could do splits; he could do spins. But the James Brown fancy steps, if you talk about that kind of thing, that was not what Jackie was into."

In his book **The Rolling Stone Illustrated History of Rock and Roll**, author Joe McEwen wrote that Jackie "dropped by" the Fox Theater in Detroit during a Dominoes rehearsal after Clyde McPhatter had left the group and boasted to Ward that he was a better singer than McPhatter. Ward auditioned him and was supposedly astonished that what Jackie claimed was actually true. While McEwan calls this story a legend, a similar but elaborated version is repeated by Newman and Kaltman based on an interview with Joyce Greenburg McRae, a friend of Jackie's. They claim Jackie was having a difficult time getting gigs when he heard Billy Ward and the Dominoes were playing at the Michigan State Fair. Jackie donned a floppy hat and "with a broad on each arm, ambled into the fair's rehearsal area and announced to Billy Ward, 'I'm Sonny Wilson.'" (The authors create a contradiction, too, in that they claim Jackie adopted the name "Sonny" to distinguish himself from another boxer from the 1940s named Jackie Wilson, but Campbell claims his family called him Sonny or Jack early on.) It was Billy Ward who convinced a reluctant young Jack to use the name Jackie Wilson.

According to Newman and Kaltman, the following conversation resulted:

"Beg your pardon," replied Ward. "Who?"

"Sonny Wilson."

"What are they for?" (He was referring to the women.)

"They're my women!"

"Well, Sonny, the two ladies have to go. And go take off that stupid hat, and when you grow up, come back in here, and I'll talk to you."

Given Ward's general demeanor as a man who broached no monkey business, Jackie must have mightily impressed him with his previously untrained singing voice, although Ward is said to have stated that Jackie sang three octaves too high for his range. It was after this incident that Ward decided Jackie could accompany the group on the tour as an "occasional participant" to gain experience.

Jackie claimed to have been influenced by Al Jolson, the Dixie Hummingbirds, Louis Jordan, the Mill Brothers and the Ink Spots— groups reputed to have sugared their acts to appeal to a white audience—and studied them with the intensity for which he later became noted himself. But Clyde McPhatter would have by far the greatest direct impact on Jackie's emerging stage and recording abilities. Jackie, in fact, admitted publicly that he had fallen in love with McPhatter's voice.

In **Nowhere to Run: The Story of Soul Music**, author Gerri Hirshey discussed McPhatter's wide range of influence on contemporaneous singers: "The list of artists who credit McPhatter as an early influence includes singers as diverse as Screamin' Jay

Hawkins, Jackie Wilson, and Smokey Robinson. The elements that would later characterize many soul acts—the emotional delivery, the gospel-oriented call-and-response patterns, even the flashy, drop-to-your-knees theatrics—all were part of McPhatter's appeal."

Twists, shimmies, and moans, Jackie obsessively absorbed McPhatter's moves and made them his own. He openly admitted his unabashed respect and admiration for Clyde McPhatter. "I learned a lot from Clyde—that high-pitched choke he used and other things. I know they say Little Richard when they say Jackie Wilson. But he did not give me anything. I like Dixie Humming-birds and Ira Tucker, who could really scream. *I Just Can't Help It* was one of his songs. I recorded it. Used Jimmy Jones, you know, the deep, deep bass voice of The Hummingbirds. I like James Cleve-land, a fine gospel singer, and recorded one of his songs, *I Don't Need You Around.* But Clyde McPhatter was my man. Clyde and Billy Ward."

Billy Ward had made a name for himself in Harlem as a gospel coach. He schooled many young men in harmonies and phrasing, often using the homes of his charges instead of having his own studio. Usually grouped as quartets, they received invitations to travel to various Baptist and Sanctified churches, and the coach acted as road manager, banker, tour guide, and surrogate parent.

Ward, whose father was a minister, was a strict disciplinarian. He had trained himself in the art of quartet singing, played the pi-ano and organ, wrote songs, and obsessed about his group's ap-pearance and comportment. While Ward groomed and preened his groups, he also studied the winds of change in pop music in the late 1940s. He saw black groups were growing in popularity and at the urging of his agent, Rose Marks, handpicked promising talent from his legion of gospel singers to form the rhythm and blues group, The Dominoes, with seventeen-year-old Clyde McPhatter as lead.

The Dominoes built their sound on classic quartet harmonies. Their lyrics ran without a hitch from praising the Lord to praising the women the Lord had created. McPhatter brought a Southern Baptist flavor to the rhythm and blues world, which was more used to lead vocalists with the detached coolness of Sonny Til. Gerri Hirshey describes rhythm and gospel as a street mongrel. But by July 1952, The Dominoes were recognized as one of the leading rhythm and blues groups. In fact, some believed they were the best when they topped the Five Keys and the Clovers in a Pittsburgh Courier poll.

Ever watchful of music's constant flux, Ward began a retreat from rhythm and blues and moved into pop standards like *These Foolish Things* and *Rags to Riches*. This trend was the result of an increasing desire of the white market for black music, or what amounted to a black shading on white standards like *Star Dust* and *Deep Purple*. This change in direction coincided with the dissatisfaction of Clyde McPhatter with many aspects of Ward's militaristic requirements. For one, McPhatter was not getting paid enough. Not surprisingly, Ward acted as paymaster, paying each Dominoe $100 per week after deducting taxes, food, and hotel charges. Anyone disobeying Ward's rules regarding appearance, tardiness, or unacceptable behavior paid a fine from what remained. The group, led by McPhatter, was becoming mutinous, and Ward is said to have fired them all at one point.

Meanwhile, McPhatter had made no secret of his intention to leave the group for a solo venture. It was for this reason that Ward called Jackie Wilson and asked him to join the group on an informal basis to allow McPhatter to groom him as his replacement.

You see, in the name "Billy Ward and His Dominoes," the word "his" says it all. The Dominoes belonged to him, day and night, seven days a week. Gerri Hirshey writes about life under Billy Ward's thumb: "The Dominoes were successful with McPhatter almost instantly. In 1951 and 1952 they had three hits, including the classic *Sixty Minute Man*. Arching his long, supple frame into a back bend, McPhatter was a box-office dream. But Billy Ward pressed his troops just a bit too hard and lost the best lead singer he could ever have had. It couldn't have sat well when Ward insisted that the Dominoes actually stand for inspection before performances. Fines were levied for lateness, for wrinkles, and for unshined shoes. On tour, under the leash of Ward's regime, McPhatter developed attitude problems that got him drummed out of the group in 1953.

The feelings may have been mutual. **The Illustrated History of Pop Music** asserts: "Ward sacked McPhatter in 1953 when group member Jackie Wilson replaced his idol as lead singer... but [he] may have felt that Wilson's near-operatic voice held better opportunities for universal appeal." Jackie, who had followed the group on tour with undisguised devotion, was most assuredly waiting in the wings.

Clyde was not only bitter about Ward's payment policy, he was also upset the rhythm and blues world thought Billy Ward was the lead singer. While Ward publicly claimed he had fired Clyde after matters "came to a head" in Providence, Rhode Island, Clyde insisted he left the group of his own volition.

Confessing years later that he had been hopelessly in love with McPhatter's voice, Jackie's love affair waned as soon as he took his place in the spotlight. Jackie's natural flamboyance was upstaging the group, and he began dropping to one knee and crooning Jolson-style to the women in the audience. Constantly watchful of the group's image, Ward admonished him to get up off his knee and sing like a man.

Despite Jackie's budding ego, he must have reasoned he needed the tutelage, coaching, and discipline of Ward to perfect his technique and style and to ultimately get where he wanted to go. "Billy was not an easy man to work for," Jackie once said, but he was quick to also point out his attributes. "He was a choral coach at Carnegie Hall. He played piano and organ, could arrange, and he was a fine director and coach. He knew what he wanted, and you had to give it to him. And he was a strict disciplinarian. You better believe it! You paid a fine if you stepped out of line. But he was a nice man. I studied under him for about two years straight, and I stayed with the Dominoes until 1956."

An isolated reference hints to a possible medical problem early in Jackie's career. In early November 1953, when the Dominoes were on tour with Sugar Ray Robinson in Charlotte, North Carolina, Jackie collapsed on stage and was rushed back to Detroit for major surgery as he had a severe case of tonsillitis and had his tonsils removed. Fortunately, this had no effect on his singing voice. But it would not be the last incident of his being carried off stage during a performance. McPhatter went off to start The Drifters, and Jackie, as lead, recorded with the Dominoes for the King and Federal labels for two years. Some of their hits included *You Can't Keep a Good Man Down* (Federal) and *Rags To Riches* (King), a #3 R&B hit in early 1954. The group recorded briefly for the Jubilee label and were then signed to the Decca label in June of 1956. Their first Decca single, *St. Therese of the Roses*, was the group's first pop chart hit and a major turning point in Jackie's career.

While Jackie is touring with the dignified Dominoes, Elvis Presley's provocative bump and grind performances were being both hailed and blasted from coast to coast. The Dominoes as a group, and Jackie in particular, were held in high regard and very popular with other vocalists of the time period. In a tape of a December 1956 jam session with Elvis Presley, Carl Perkins, and Jerry Lee Lewis, Elvis raves about Jackie's stage performance. But Jackie felt stifled because, like McPhatter before him, people thought he was Ward. Jackie, undoubtedly aware of Elvis's rapidly spreading fame, knew he wanted to go solo.

There were warning signs early on that the Dominoes were only a stepping stone for Jackie. Between 1951 and 1954, Ruth Brown—

The Girl With The Tear In Her Voice—was the top selling black female singer in the U.S. In her autobiography, **Miss Rhythm**, Ruth Brown relates an incident that occurred when she first met Jackie, right after he replaced McPhatter. Jackie offered to buy her a drink and came close to being fired from the Dominoes because of it. When the band's manager and songwriter, Rose Marks, read Jackie the riot act in front of everyone, Ruth writes, "that was the beginning of the end as far as Jackie was concerned."

Ward replaced Jackie with Eugene Mumford, formerly of the Larks, the Golden Gate Quartet and the Serenaders. The parting must have been amicable because Ward continued as Jackie's manager, booking him in clubs that would provide Jackie with the exposure he would need for the next step on his journey to stardom.

Chapter Two

Rock My Soul
You Can't Keep a Good Man Down

Growing up in Detroit when he did had much to do with Jackie Wilson's eventual success. Next to Chicago, Motor City had the largest black population of any American city, growing from 5,000 in 1910 to more than 80,000 by 1926. This was largely due to blacks from the South heading north to work in factories, and the Detroit auto works provided many jobs for blacks during this period. By the 1950s, black life was firmly entrenched in neighborhoods like Jackie's and black music, coalescing as an urban adaptation of southern gospel, began to grow and flourish. In the national arena, however, there were two kinds of music—black music and white music. There was nothing in between, and no song or artist spanned the expansive gulf between them.

"Race music," as defined by whites in the 1920s, came into being when black vaudeville artist Mamie Smith recorded *Crazy Blues*. The term soon became a catchall phrase for any kind of music done by a black artist. By the time World War II came and went and many black soldiers had given their lives in the peace effort, people became more sensitive to the issues of race and equality. ***Billboard*** magazine had a chart heading entitled "Top 15 Best Selling Race Records" and substituted the less pejorative but stereotypical "rhythm and blues" in June 1949. Rhythm and blues then became a substitute catchall for black music no matter what the stripe—jazz, folk, pop, or big band. If the artists were black, it must be rhythm and blues.

About rhythm and blues, in his book **Honkers and Shouters: The Golden Years of Rhythm & Blues**, Arnold Shaw writes: "R&B was liberated music, which in its pristine form represented a break with white, mainstream pop. Developing from black sources, it embodied the fervor of gospel music, the throbbing vigor of boogie woogie, the jump beat of swing, and the gutsiness and sexuality of life in the black ghetto."

Despite the rise of independent record labels that began recording artists like Cecil Gant and a favorite of Jackie's, Louis Jordan, known as the Father of Rhythm and Blues, most early black music was a group phenomenon for cultural and social reasons. When Johnny Otis introduced Jackie Wilson to Ralph Bass at King Records in 1951, Bass passed him up in favor of a group sound— the Dominoes. The reason for his rejection did not go unnoticed by Jackie.

During this time most whites had never heard of rhythm and blues, much less actually listened to it, and it was equally shunned by upper class blacks as trash music. A few white disk jockeys were weaving rhythm and blues recordings into their radio programs across the nation, but generally the belief existed among radio station program directors that mixing white and black music would result in the alienation of both audiences: a sure recipe for financial failure. Still, some outstanding rhythm and blues singles did breach the cultural brick wall and began appearing on the nation's white pop charts, proving whites were finally listening to, and buying, black music.

Around 1950, a radio station in Memphis woke up to the fact that blacks had established their own considerable buying power, estimated to be $100 million in that city with a national potential approaching $10 to 12 billion. The previously all-white station WDIA began broadcasting "forbidden" music, turning over half the station's programming to gospel. WDIA achieved instant success with Memphis listeners, among them the fourteen-year-old Elvis Presley.

A style of music called rhythm and blues (R&B), with its guttural sounds and earthy subject matter, was anathema to the white American adult. Their rejection made it absolutely acceptable to America's white youth, and this generation's alienation would eventually influence the direction aspiring young white musicians would take.

Disk jockey and music promoter Alan Freed is most often credited with introducing black music to young whites in the early to mid-1950s. But according to John A. Jackson, a Freed biographer, the story upon which this credit is based is untrue, or at least, embellished. Alan Freed was a popular deejay in Cleveland during this time. Leo Mintz, a record store owner, catered in part to Cleveland's large black population. On the strength of his sales, Mintz persuaded Freed to add rhythm and blues tunes to his classical program on the local AM radio station WJW.

Freed was perhaps groomed to be a bridge between the races. As a boy, his best friend was black, and Freed endured and learned to ignore racial slurs and bigoted attitudes. Despite hate letters branding him as a nigger-lover, Freed began to mix rhythm and blues recordings into his radio program. Young whites who had not yet formed cultural and musical prejudices started eavesdropping on the music of the many talented black singers and musicians of the day. Likewise, young white musicians, casting about for role models, were inspired and influenced by the talent of their black contemporaries. Music marketers, ever watchful of what young people were spending their disposable income on, saw that rhythm and blues was playing a role in developing musical preferences of everyone. The seeds that would blossom into rock and roll were sown.

But first there would be "grey music" crossovers, i.e., black music designed to appeal to whites and vice versa. The term "blue-eyed soul" was coined by a good friend of Jackie's, a black disk jockey in Philadelphia named George Woods, to describe the Righteous Brothers, whose records were aired on rhythm and blues radio by black disk jockeys before they knew "The Brothers" were actually white. Many rhythm and blues groups became popular with both races strictly on their merits as talented performers. Others, like the Ink Spots and the Mills Brothers, found the middle road easier and sweetened their sound to appeal to white palates. *Sixty Minute Man,* which was recorded by the Dominoes in the summer of 1951, was the first true rhythm and blues record to cross over to the national pop charts, and Jackie would adapt his style to this white/ black paradigm for the rest of his performing career. Besides the mid-century change in racial views, a profound technological change widened the rhythm and blues highway. In 1946 the Federal Communications Commission allowed area radio stations to occupy the same or adjacent frequencies in a given area. The proliferation of radio stations resulted in greater music diversity. Two stations in the South, WLAC in Nashville and WDIA in Memphis, played the greatest role. WLAC had high-wattage broadcast power that reached thousands of listeners. "Daddy" Gene Nobles and later "John R" Richbourg, both white deejays at WLAC, played jump band jazz and Count Basie tunes. When they began to receive requests for rhythm and blues recordings made in the South, the deejays gave their listeners what they craved. Richbourg claimed to have given Jackie his first national radio play.

In fact, music would be the vehicle to crash through the brick wall that stood between the races. Alan Freed, corralling the talents of Billy Ward and his Dominoes and other equally gifted black groups through many concerts and armory performances around the country, would become the pied piper of tolerance as young people of both races tossed off their prejudices and got down and dirty on the dance floor.

For black musicians, personal appearances were especially important because the record industry had acquired the habit of not paying them royalties. Consequently, they derived most of their income from touring. On June 5, 1953, Billy Ward and his Dominoes, starring their new lead singer, "Sonny" Wilson, played at a rhythm and blues dance with ex-heavyweight boxing champion Joe Louis and his band, and Bill Haley and His Comets. At the Akron Armory on August 14th, Freed showcased the Dominoes as the lead group, which marked the beginning of a lifelong friendship between Freed and Wilson. Freed would later be credited with giving Jackie the moniker "Mr. Excitement." Christmas night, 1953, the Dominoes, headlining with Little Walter and His Jukes and the Ralph Williams Orchestra, played to a crowd of 3,000 after 2,500 had been turned away at the door.

Freed, known to Cleveland audiences by his radio persona "Moondog," was on the cutting edge of where music was headed in the 1950s. When he moved to WINS in New York, the name Moondog was already in use, so Freed christened his new radio show the "Rock and Roll Party." When reminded that the phrase "rock & roll" was a black term for sex, Freed is quoted as saying "I don't give a shit; that's what I am going to call the show!" Freed is generally credited with coining the term "rock & roll," though he initially insisted it was only meant as a name for his show featuring rhythm and blues. By 1961, he was assuming full credit for giving rock 'n roll its name.

Despite Freed's contention, the words rock and roll were entwining themselves together without his help. While the two-word phrase shows up repeatedly in rhythm and blues songs, each word was used individually and interchangeably as early as the 1920s to denote intercourse. Before long, however, rock 'n roll took on a non-sexual connotation as the world became receptive to a new music form that combined the best of both the white and black musical cultures, and it is upon this stage that Elvis Presley and Jackie Wilson entered the music scene.

Whether from parental and societal pressures or mere teen fickleness and thirst for new experience, white audiences could not digest a full plate of rhythm and blues. Though black music had started the revolution of youth culture in the early 1950s, its prominence lasted only until white culture cultivated heroes of its own. The next step in the progression occurred when Paul Anka led the white teen idol phase with *Diana* in 1957. Dick Clark's American Bandstand appeared on American television in 1957 and at forty million daily viewers, reached the largest music audience in history. Clark's uncanny vision of the future of rock & roll prompted his creation of the white teen idol phenomenon that brought white middle class respectability to sounds that had been called "gutbucket blues" thirty years earlier.

Freed, every bit as savvy a promoter and prognosticator as Dick Clark, also proved correct in his vision of how rock & roll would progress when songs by white rock & rollers Buddy Holly, Jerry Lee Lewis and the Everly Brothers appeared at the top of the pop charts in 1957. In fact, the mid-fifties, the formative years of rock 'n roll, showed the business end of the record industry that American kids were growing up to be voracious consumers of sound—from rhythm and blues grit to soft doowop, hard-charging Ray Charles to Elvis' white-boy blues. Large metropolitan areas developed their own styles based on the demands of their growing radio listeners and concert-goers. Urban rock and roll radio remained largely black, with the exception of Bill Haley, until Elvis appeared in early 1956. It was in Detroit's Motor City, the home of soul, that Berry Gordy, Jr., would write Jackie Wilson's first singles hit.

Jackie must have sensed he was headed for the top and that remaining the unbilled lead for the Dominoes would not get him there. He knew to get noticed he would have to break away and go solo. Between February and June of 1957, Jackie was booked to perform at several Detroit clubs including Lee's Club Sensation and The Flame Show Bar as a supporting act to the quintessential jazz singer, Miss Billie Holiday. Already well known from his stint with the Dominoes, Jackie's performances drew immediate notice, especially by Billy Davis, who was writing songs with Gordy under the name Tyran Carlo and his partner Rose Marks. They saw the potential in Jackie and introduced him to Al Green.

Berry Gordy, Jr., like Jackie, was a boxer in Detroit in his early years. He was also just starting and trying to make a name for himself as a songwriter. In his autobiography, **To Be Loved,** Gordy talks about the time his sister Gwen, who worked in the Flame Show Bar, made the connection that would transform their lives.

"The night Gwen introduced me to Al Green was a big one for me. Besides owning the club, he managed a few singers—Johnny Ray, LaVern Baker and a guy he had just signed by the name of Jackie Wilson. Al told me he also owned a music publishing company and was always looking for new material and told me to stop by his office with some of my songs."

Green had been following Jackie's career since the Dominoes's days and had made it known he was impressed. When he heard Gordy's songs, he saw a match made in heaven.

For **In the Groove: The People Behind the Music**, Ted Fox interviewed Bob Thiele, founder of the successful independent jazz recording company, Signature. Thiele was also known for his role in convincing the Decca label to release Buddy Holly's early hits on their Coral label. Besides recording Jackie's debut hits on Brunswick, he recorded Pat Boone, Lawrence Welk, Steve Allen, Louis Armstrong and Duke Ellington.

Fox: I'm surprised that Brunswick was considered a "B" label. For me, Jackie Wilson was the great Brunswick star. How did he come to your attention?

Thiele: In those days what would happen is, you'd get a call from Al Green, and he'd say "I'd like to come by and play you some music, and introduce you to some of my acts." And that was our job. We saw the people who had reputations and could present some new talent for us. So he came in and he had a vocal group he wanted to sell me, the Dominoes. So I went to the Apollo Theatre one night to hear them. I saw Jackie Wilson with the Dominoes and

I said to myself, "To hell with the Dominoes, let's take Jackie Wilson. " In those days there were a lot of cutthroat approaches to things, I admit. I said to Al Green, "I don't want to sign a vocal group, but I'd like to sign the kid." Well, you know, all he saw were the dollar signs and he said, "I don't care about the vocal group either. Take Jackie Wilson, you got him."

But the deal did not go down without further cutting of throats. The man who would do much of the arranging for Brunswick, Dick Jacobs, recalled that Jackie was nothing more than a trading chip for bigger stakes. In a **Musician** article entitled "Jackie Wilson: Taking It Higher: A Producer Remembers Mr. Excitement" by Dick Jacobs as told to Tim Holmes, Jacobs said: "Bob got in touch with Al Green to talk about the contract. Green told Thiele that Coral/ Brunswick could have [LaVern] Baker at the end of her then-current contract, which had another year to run. The deal was contingent on one condition: that the label agree to a package deal and sign another young singer Green had under contract. His name was Jackie Wilson, a virtual unknown who'd been with Billy Ward & the Dominoes. Green wanted to launch the kid on a solo career and part of the package was that we record him immediately. Ironically, while we waited for LaVern Baker's contract to run out, Green died, and we never got to record her. Instead, Jackie Wilson became a major figure in rock 'n roll history.

"We'd heard Jackie sing on his Billy Ward sides and knew he had some vocal chops. But those tracks had been recorded some time back, and we weren't sure how Jackie would fly solo. One day Thiele called me in and said that Jackie was coming in for the first sessions. 'Probably by freight train,' he semi-joked. We'd have to cut Jackie fast since he didn't have the money to stay in New York for any extended period. Since time was tight, I was concerned about the songs we'd be recording. Jackie was bringing in a couple of tunes penned by Berry Gordy, Jr. Not only was the singer an unknown, but who the hell ever heard of the songwriter?"

You have to wonder whether Jackie knew about the sleight of hand going on behind his back. You also have to wonder why the record company could not (or would not) pay to put him up in a hotel and feed him while they ironed out their package deal. Brunswick had once handled stars Bing Crosby and Louis Armstrong, but was dormant at the time in question. Regardless, Thiele completes the drama as Jackie is passed like so much property into new hands during December, 1957: "So, I'll never forget, Al Green was staying at the Taft Hotel in New York, and I wanted to get the contract signed. He had had it a couple of days, and I was to pick it up at his hotel one morning. So I rang the room and a young man got on, a kid eighteen or nineteen years old, and he says, 'Mr. Green died last night. ' I said 'Oh, my God, that's terrible!' He said, 'But I have a contract here that I was supposed to give you this morning.' So he came down and gave me the contract. And that kid was a fellow named Nat Tarnopol, who later became Jackie Wilson's manager. He even wound up at Brunswick because Decca—after I had left the company—in an attempt to keep Jackie Wilson, gave him the label. They gave him Brunswick;

that was part of the deal."

When Jackie arrived at the Pythian Temple on West 70th Street in Manhattan for his first Brunswick recoding session, he made a horrific first impression. Jacobs described his attire as old jeans and a sweatshirt that looked like they'd been slept in, as if Jackie was some bedraggled hobo off a freight train as Thiele had warned. There may be some truth in their so-called joke. If Brunswick wouldn't pay for a hotel, and Jackie couldn't afford one, perhaps he paid his own way to New York via freight train because it was cheap. Freight trains don't usually sport dining cars and sleeping coaches. If that's the case, and there is probably no one who knows for sure, then Jackie should have gotten a fair warning about the kind of treatment he would be getting for the rest of his indentured servitude to Brunswick.

Jacobs noted afterward that Jackie's appearance that day was totally out of character. Jackie's normal attire and pompadour hair-style was the height of trendy nattiness and he would never appear in public, "unless every tonsorial detail were sculpted and perfect. He was the only guy I ever knew who could spend hours in shoe stores. Yet, on this first meeting, he looked like just another kid off the street."

Jacobs' secondary impression was no better. When he asked Jackie for lead sheets of the songs he wanted to record, Jackie hadn't brought any and told Jacobs to write them down as he sang them. "I'd been down this road before with other vocalists," Jacobs re-called in Jackie Wilson: Taking It Higher: A Producer Remembers

Mr. Excitement', ". . . as I wrote out the music for Berry Gordy's *Reet Petite* I began to feel some respect for the unknown tune smith. *Reet Petite* had an unusual melody and a strikingly inventive chord construction; even before recording it, it felt like a new kind of hit.

"After I'd written down the music, Jackie and I sat down to figure out what keys to record in. I began playing piano chords in what I considered the usual male keys, but Jackie kept telling me to take it higher. I transposed the keys until they hit the female range, a full octave above where we'd started. Jackie explained that since he had laryngitis he couldn't sing along, but kept saying "take it higher" in a gravely phlegm-filled voice. I had no idea what he'd sound like in these upper-register helium arrangements he insisted on." Jacobs described how Jackie's untested voice was not setting much of a precedent for a successful recording session. Worried they'd signed a "lemon", he expressed his fears to Thiele. Thiele was fatalistic. They had only signed Jackie to keep LaVern Baker, already a proven hit maker with Atlantic Records as '"The High Priestess of Rock and Roll", and told Jacobs just to do what the kid wanted and not to worry about it.

Jacobs, although duly impressed with *Reet Petite* was truly concerned the session would turn out to be a flop, so he hedged his bet by hiring some big guns for backup- Panama Francis on drums, Lloyd Trotman on bass, Ernie Hayes on piano, Sam Taylor on saxophone and Eric Gale on guitar. This would turn out to be one of music history's most ironic decisions. When Jackie's larynx recovered and he was able to get some sleep, he showed these staid, New

York pros a thing or two.

Jacobs remembered the sensation of hearing Jackie sing for the first time at the now infamous recording session: "Jackie Wilson opened his mouth and out poured that sound like honey on moonbeams and it was like the whole room shifted on some weird axis. The musicians, these meat-and-potatoes pros, stared at each other slack-jawed and goggle-eyed in disbelief; it was as if the purpose of their musical training and woodshedding and lick-splitting had been to guide them into this big studio in the Pythian Temple to experience these pure shivering moments of magic. Bob Thiele and I looked at each other and just started laughing, half out of relief and half out of wonder. I never thought crow could taste so sweet. For years afterwards, Jackie and I often joked about my initial underestimation of his range. In fact, his vocal spread encompassed so many octaves that he could sing not only in female keys but an octave higher without a hint of a strained falsetto. *Reet Petite* came out and did very well, although nothing like the hits that would follow."

Reet Petite was released on September 8, 1957. Gordy recalls from his autobiography, "Though I would go on to have many exciting times in my life, the release of our first record on Jackie Wilson ranks among the top. Jackie took *Reet Petite*, a so-so song, and turned it into a classic . . . when I heard Joltin' Joe Howard from WCBH say, 'And now folks, the hottest new record in the land—*Reet Petite* by Jackie Wilson,' I was thrilled. Turning the volume up as loud as I could, I danced around the room. Passing the TV set, I turned on American Bandstand. Shock! There it was again! Jackie's big booming voice blasting for millions all over the country, and all those white kids dancing up a storm to my song."

There's nothing like the first time.

Record trade magazines of the day reported that the twenty-three-year-old Jackie was "hot property," having signed an exclusive disking pact with Brunswick and a booking pact with Universal Attractions Agency in September 1957. Universal announced he would perform in clubs in Washington and Pittsburgh, for disk-hops in Cleveland and in Las Vegas in November, just when Elvis's *Jailhouse Rock* LP and movie were being released.

Reet Petite was regarded as a novelty. Critics called it many things—up-tempo and high-spirited with an unbelievable range of vocal sounds. Some called the arrangement dated and accused Jackie of a shameless parody of Elvis. An article entitled "UK Fans Go Wild for Jackie's US Flop!" quoted reviewer Keith Fordyce: "a gimmick-laden disc that combines pep, beat, and originality with an irresistible go." It wasn't quite irresistible enough, only reaching #67 in the United States, but it did better with British fans reaching #6 in the United Kingdom. Fordyce's colleague Derek Johnson was not sure *Reet Petite* was destined for the hit parade. He thought Dick Jacob's "seasoned pros" sounded like a "strange collection of noises, ranging from gargling to an outboard motor . . ."

There is some credence to this opinion. *Reet Petite (The Finest Girl You Ever Want to Meet)* was inventive and original, with an unusual style written by budding songwriters, sung by a budding singer and seasoned with professional understanding. This new-ness by itself is not new, it is just that the underlying talent was so extraordinary that it got noticed by a budding record industry just beginning to realize there was a lot of money to be made from a wealthy postwar country with a growing taste for music of almost any flavor. Whether you like its sounds and subtleties or not, *Reet Petite* grabs your ear, and that was all the twenty-three-year-old Jackie Wilson needed to get him on the music map.

Chapter Three

Taking It Higher

The same day Berry Gordy found himself dancing around his living room listening to his song being featured on *American Bandstand*, he called Jackie Wilson eager to discuss their next song, a slow ballad called *To Be Loved*. Nevertheless, Jackie, already a star in the making, could not be found, even by his manager Nat Tarnopol. A few days later, Jackie showed up at Gordy's doorstep, according to Gordy, "with his pretty-boy face and pretty-boy hair, a doo with an upswept pompadour in front, and a tight-fitting tailored suit," wanting to know what was so urgent.

Gordy had not had time to become accustomed to the aura of success but it was obvious to him Jackie had and that he wanted to cut to the bottom line—the business of hearing his next hit. Knowing Jackie was a master of quick decisions, Gordy knew he had to get his attention in the first few bars or his beloved song would be rejected.

Gordy writes, "I jumped into it, playing my usual simple chords on the piano, but singing with great soul and conviction. Even in my squeaky voice, it was easy to hear the deep passion I had for this song, singing for all I was worth, hoping he wouldn't stop me before the first hook. He didn't. I made it through the whole first verse. Great. But just as I was getting ready to start the second he said 'Okay, Okay, hold it! That's enough.'

"'Gimme that paper,' he said, grabbing the lyric sheet off the piano. 'I got it. I got it!' Circling his pointed finger at me, he said, 'Play, play.'

". . . Jackie had fallen in love with the song. And I fell in love with his dynamic voice all over again the minute he sang the first few words.

"I had never heard him do a ballad before. His voice was strong and deep and sincere. It was as if he had written it for himself. He brought up the entire range of emotions I had felt the night I wrote it. My tears came again and everything."

Because Dick Jacobs was conducting the television show *Hit Parade* at the time of Jackie's second recording session, Milton Delugg substituted as director and arranger. *To Be Loved*, along with *I'm Wanderin'* and *Danny Boy,* were recorded with swirling strings and orchestral backup in an attempt to highlight Jackie's incredible range and versatility. In May of 1958, while Elvis was ensconced in basic training with the Army at Fort Hood, Texas, Jackie's *To Be Loved* reached #7 in the R&B charts but only rose as far as #22 in the US and UK pop charts. Unlike Elvis, Jackie would never be required to serve in the military, because he was married with a child and another on the way, causing a hardship on his wife, Freda.

To Be Loved is a powerful song due to the combination of Jackie's voice and the strong orchestral arrangement, but some critics panned it as heavy-handed, claiming the piece was "melodramatic." Time has proven *To Be Loved* a classic piece of music given the musical tastes in vogue at the time it was produced. Using the songs from this session, Jackie released his first album, *He's So Fine*, the following October, but it failed to chart.

Still looking for that big hit, Jackie was set to record his third session in Detroit at the United Sound Studio. Raynoma Gordy Singleton, in her autobiography entitled **Berry, Me and Motown,** describes the scene when Jackie arrived to rehearse *Lonely Teardrops*. "For weeks now, all I'd heard was Jackie Wilson, Jackie Wilson. And it was no wonder that Berry had such high regard for him. For a guy to take your songs and do them the justice that Jackie had done Berry's work, you had to love the man. When Jackie strutted into the house that morning, the place stopped. What a sight: his perfected 'do' and his shimmering shirt unbuttoned to the navel. Diamond rings and gold chains. Major flash and personality. His mere presence shouted out 'Jackie's here!'

"As Berry and the other guys swarmed around him, hand-slapping and calling out a 'Hey, man', I stood to the side. Even from that distance, I could see that the reports I'd heard were true: Jackie never went anywhere without makeup. His was a thick pancake foundation with eyeliner and rouge, maybe a touch of lipstick, I thought. It was a practice, I understood, he shared with many of his peers. There was something both ludicrous and then completely appropriate about it, a way to call attention to themselves as stars."

According to Raynoma, *Lonely Teardrops* had been intended for another artist Gordy worked with named Eddie Holland, the brother of one of the Satintones. Although Eddie lacked Jackie's vocal range, his version of the song *Jamie* was as similar to Jackie's voice as Terry Stafford's was to Elvis in his early 1960s hit, *Suspicion*. Eddie had done a demo of *Lonely Teardrops* but it was performed languorously, more ballad-like. Because the cha-cha was a popular dance at the time, Jackie picked up the tempo and, with Gordy and Davis directing, produced a demo of what would become his signature song.

In Tim Holmes' **Musician** article, Dick Jacobs relates how Jackie's demo, and Gordy himself, ended up with him in New York. "Nat told me that in the future I would be Jackie's sole arranger, and that he and I would co-produce on the sessions. He handed me a lead sheet for another Berry Gordy composition, *Lonely Teardrops,* and asked me to call Gordy in Detroit to discuss the arrangement. This would be the first of many phone calls over the years, but this time I had some questions. The chord progression of *Lonely Teardrops* struck me as being a little unusual, and I asked Gordy if it were correct. He assured me that it was and we went on to discuss the arrangement in highly technical terms. Not only was Gordy a budding populist genius in terms of knowing the teen market, he was a brilliant and knowledgeable music theorist. The phone conversation ended with me inviting Gordy to New York for the *Lonely Teardrops* session. Jackie often had a slightly different slant on certain events of his own life. In his interview with Norman Knight he said of *Lonely Teardrops*, "Well, it's an old story but a good one. The truth of the matter is it was supposed to be a ballad, a blues ballad, and it was also written by Berry Gordy, Jr. Nat and I flew in from New York and we liked it and took it back. Then we did record it as a blues ballad but we didn't like it. So then we decided to play with the guitar a little bit. We had a great arranger at the time, Dick Jacobs. We had him finagle with it a little bit and we played and we got a good tempo going. It was a calypso at the time. Which was very popular and we took it, and we liked it. We brought it back; we gave it to the disc jockey. It was hot off the press and we told him to play it. So they put the record on and Berry was waiting patiently and everybody was just waiting and they put it on. Berry said, 'Oh my God! You've ruined my record, my song, what have you done!' Tears came out of his eyes."

Gordy must have shed many teardrops over the songs he composed for Jackie. Sometimes they were tears of joy, sometimes not.

In their demo, Gordy and Davis relied more heavily on Jackie's voice than on backup instruments. They abandoned strings and brass opting for drums, electric bass, baritone sax, and what would later become Gordy's signature sound—the tambourine. Gordy's instinct for giving music buyers what they wanted was proven at last. After all the near misses, *Lonely Teardrops* topped ***Billboard's*** R&B chart for 22 weeks at the end of 1958. On the pop chart it reached #7, making it Jackie's first crossover hit and sealing his fame as a rock 'n roll star. The following February, over a million copies of *Lonely Teardrops* had been snatched up by his growing legion of fans, earning him his first gold record. In contrast, by this time Elvis already had twenty-one gold singles and five gold albums.

Jackie's rise to stardom was accelerated by back-to-back live performances booked for him while his records were hitting the airwaves and record stores. He appeared twice on Dick Clark's **American Bandstand** singing *To Be Loved* and *We Have Love*. Record trade publications announced that after playing to a packed house in October 1958, Jackie was signed for a return engagement at the Apollo Theater in New York in December. In the remaining days of October, he played the Howard Theater in Washington, D.C., Baltimore's Royal Theater and on October 24th, joined LaVern Baker, Bobby Day, Lee Andrews & the Hearts, and the Arnett Cobb orchestra in a six-week series of one-nighters around the East. Long known as the original hardest working man in show business, a certified workaholic by today's standards, Jackie did not go home for holidays. On Christmas day, 1958 he began a ten-day session in Alan Freed's Rock 'n Roll Spectacular at Loew's State Theater, New York, alongside sixteen other acts including Eddie Cochran, Bo Diddley, and The Everly Brothers. While in New York for that gig, he appeared on **The Dick Clark Show** on ABC-TV with Jill Corey, Jimmy Clanton, The Crests, and Ritchie Valens.

In the spring of 1959, he continued his marathon pace, appearing again on **The Dick Clark Show** and Freed's ten-day Easter pageant at the Brooklyn Fox Theater in March. The month of May finds Jackie headlining at the Greystone Ballroom and then heading for Hollywood. June 3rd he performed with Jerry Lee Lewis and a large revue in Charlotte, North Carolina and scurried to New Orleans for a June 9th performance at the Coliseum Arena on his 25th birthday. During the second half of 1959 he appeared twice on *The Dick Clark Show*, headlined The Biggest Show of Stars for "59" at the Municipal Auditorium, New Orleans, and appeared as a special guest at the Copa Club in Newport, Kentucky, for five days in December. He ended 1959 by headlining Alan Freed's "Big Beat Show" at the Brooklyn Fox on December 29th.

The debut of Freed's Rock 'n Roll Spectacular coincided with the scheduling of the production of his new movie, *Go, Johnny Go* starring Chuck Berry, Jimmy Clanton, the Cadillacs, Eddie Cochran, Harvey Fuqua, and the Moonglows among others, with Jackie scheduled to sing *Lonely Teardrops* and *You Better Know It.* Only *You Better Know It* made it to the big screen.

According to Bill Millar, who wrote the jacket notes for the Ace re-release of *Reet Petite* in 1984, "His back flips, pretty footwork and legendary sexuality brought comparisons with Elvis and almost as much criticism. 'What mother,' wrote one lady in a letter to Soul, 'Would let her daughter see Jackie Wilson? He puts on one of the most obscene performances I've ever seen in my life. If people were supposed to act like that man does in public, then we wouldn't wear clothes and have our own houses. Everyone would just run around nude and party in the streets. I suggest you quit running stories and pictures on that man until he either cleans up his act or quits singing altogether. To think white people got upset over Elvis Presley.'"

Jackie might have been pleased to have been compared in any fashion to Elvis, already a millionaire and working on his fifth movie, but he received not a cent to suffer the irate protestations of mothers. In a telling example of the kind of mind-set taking shape behind the sound mixers and microphones, the musicians received no money for movie performances. Unless given a speaking part, like Chuck Berry in this case, musicians were expected to be happy with exposure as their sole reward.

Songwriters got even less, and everyone involved in Jackie's recordings at this time concur on what happened. Gordy recalled that despite the success of all five of their songs to date, he had very little to show for it. It seemed no one was making any money but the record companies. Raynoma's version of what happened went like this: . . . when I found out what slick-talking, hotshot Nat Tarnopol was paying Berry for all the Jackie Wilson hits, my fighting spirit was inflamed.

"The best Nat could offer was an intermittent, nominal advance of fifty or seventy-five dollars, or the loan of a car. For any more, Tarnopol would shrug as if to say, 'So sue me,' and point Berry to the door. It seemed to burn me more than it did Berry. We couldn't continue to be a little school of black guppies swimming in a sea of white sharks."

Gordy's explanation went into greater detail, "They paid us all right. But only for the A-side, our song, the song that people heard on the radio and asked for in stores." Gordy described how Nat Tarnopol, labeled a notorious tightwad by Raynoma, used songs written by a relative or someone he owed a favor to on the B-side, and that these freeloaders received the same amount of money and benefited from their association with the A-side hit. When Gordy confronted Nat, he blurted out a spur-of-the moment, hardly-contemplated ultimatum . . . either they were given the B-side or they would not write for Jackie.

Nat was unimpressed, telling Gordy Jackie was a star, that they needed Jackie more than Jackie needed them. Gordy left, telling Nat they were through, but then sought out Jackie both to tell him about his argument with Nat and in hopes Jackie might be able to smooth things over. Jackie told Gordy he loved him and his songs but he had to stick with his management.

Billy Davis said of the breakup, "We stopped writing and confronted Nat about paying us, either for producer or something, or at least to give us the B-sides on the records. It was a singles market then and getting the B-sides was very important financially, and Nat always reserved the B-side for his interests. Nat wouldn't hear of it. He said, hey, if you don't like what I'm doing, then leave; I'll go find other writers. He always talked and walked like he owned the world. So we did leave, and that turned out to be the best thing for both Berry and I."

Dick Jacobs in Tim Holmes' *Musician* article claims the flip-side of *Lonely Teardrops* tells the story going on behind the scenes.

"The new head of A&R at Coral/Brunswick, Paul Cohen, came from the country department at Decca. To put it charitably, Cohen and Tarnopol hated each other with a passion. Cohen always wanted one of his, or one of his friends' songs on every session, and Tarnopol objected vehemently. Cohen won the battle, if not the war, by issuing Nat a simple ultimatum: Unless the flip of *Lonely Teardrops* was an old ballad called *In the Blue of Evening,* there'd be no session. Nat was furious and came up with an ingenious sabotage scheme. He told me to deliberately write the arrangement in the wrong key for Jackie. That way, *In the Blue of Evening* would get so screwed up that we could pull one of Jackie's older sides for the flip.

"The scheme would have worked had it not been for Jackie. I wrote the arrangement in what I thought was an impossible key. Jackie, unaware of the subterfuge, took the arrangement and—without breaking a quaver—turned out such a beautiful performance that we were forced to use *In the Blue of Evening*. His rendition of this smoldering chestnut of a tune was the first clue we had to the incredible versatility of his singing."

This incident would become a decisive fork in the road for both Gordy and Jackie: Gordy's Motown Records empire would ultimately alter the course of American music history, and Jackie's loyalty to Nat would set a career-long precedent of allowing his management to put their own interests ahead of his.

I'll Be Satisfied, which reached to #20 on the US pop charts, was the last hit written for Jackie by Gordy and Davis. Gordy was a smart and talented man with good partners. Once they got over the shock of Gordy telling Nat and Jackie good bye, Gordy's sister, Gwen, and Smokey Robinson convinced him they would be better off starting a record company on their own. After all, wasn't that where all the money was? Raynoma apparently sided with the rest: "So, why, I reasoned, should we continue to give Nat Tarnopol and Jackie Wilson our best material, all for their benefit? We had other avenues. And Nat's attitude—that songwriters were at the bottom of the totem pole—was insulting. Anybody could write a song, Nat implied, and we should be happy having his star Jackie recording our stuff. Regardless of the pittance of a royalty he paid when and if he paid."

Name a prominent black star or group and they probably fell under Gordy's tutelage and autocracy at some point. Gordy would fundamentally determine the sound of the sixties, molding budding as well as established talent into the Motown sound—the Supremes, the Jackson 5, Martha Reeves and the Vandellas, Gladys Knight and the Pips, the Temptations, the Four Tops, Stevie Wonder and Junior Walker are a partial list. He liked to tell interviewers, "The Motown sound is made up of rats, roaches, and love." The proof of Gordy's acumen was in the numbers: 110 hits in *Billboard's* pop Top Ten between 1961 and 1971. Of Jackie Wilson's influence he wrote: "Jackie Wilson was the epitome of natural greatness. Unfortunately for some, he set the standard I would be looking for in artists forever."

Though Jackie's influence on Gordy reverberated into many of

Motown's stars, Michael Jackson's stage performance is the best example. *In To Be Loved,* Gordy recalled: "He (Michael Jackson) then moved to center stage for a solo spot with his latest hit, Billy Jean. He had touches of many of the greats in that one performance—Sammy Davis, Jr., Fred Astaire, Jackie Wilson, Marcel Marceau, and James Brown. But it was his own Moonwalk that blew everybody away." Gordy's Motown Records would ultimately become the most successful black-owned record company, not to mention one of the most successful black-owned corporations in USA history. Not bad for the son of Georgia farmers who migrated to Detroit in 1922 to escape an epidemic of black lynchings.

Meanwhile, Alan Freed was engaged in a frenzy of rock 'n roll promotions around the country in armories and dance halls, wherever he could attract a crowd with big-name, up-and-coming talent. On March 27, 1959, he began a ten-day show full of artists eager to promote their new releases. Among them were headliner Fats Domino, teen idols Bobby Darin and Fabian, and Jackie Wilson singing *That's Why (I Love You So).* By May, *That's Why (I Love You So)* had climbed to US #13.

According to author John A. Jackson in his book **Big Beat Heat**, sometime that same spring Freed staged a Jackie Wilson marathon on his radio show. "Although Wilson's manager also worked for Roulette Records, Ray Reneri [Freed's assistant] said, 'No one knew what Alan's association was with Jackie.' But Freed and Wilson had a close personal friendship that extended to the singer's early days with Billy Ward's Dominoes. Freed vigorously promoted

Jackie's records and personal appearances and at the time had all the more reason to do so. ***Go, Johnny, Go***, with Jackie as one of the film's featured performers, was about to be released in movie theaters across the country. What is more, Jackie's latest record, *I'll Be Satisfied*, had just been released. Freed, with the opportunity to simultaneously promote his own movie and Jackie's career, played *I'll Be Satisfied* and then asked his listeners to call and voice their opinions on the song. Freed then told his audience that since they liked Jackie's new record so much, 'We're going to play it again.' Then, said Reneri, 'He played it for 45 minutes straight and the station manager freaked.'"

Freed took some heat from WABC for this intrepid gimmick, but it was merely a tiny bubble in a large, boiling caldron. Outside the music world, the New York Grand Jury ended its session on June 10, 1959, after hearing closed-door testimony from 150 witnesses on the rigging of television quiz shows. Although the judge presiding over the hearing initially ruled that the jury's reports remain sealed, the jury was outraged by the revelations of scandal, and the report was turned over to Representative Oren Harris of Arkansas, chairman of the House Subcommittee on Legislative Oversight. It was not long before the public would get a healthy dose of scandal with both television and then the broadcasting and record industries. Many heads would roll, Alan Freed's among them, but unfortunately for talented musicians like Jackie Wilson, many of the guilty were spared and left to continue on their crooked ways unmolested.

In late 1959 Alan Freed was fired from WABC for refusing to sign an affidavit denying he accepted payola from record companies for playing their records on the air. Soon he would find himself heavily embroiled in allegations of impropriety for his association with mob-owned Roulette Records. Legal battles notwithstanding, Freed continued to do what he did best. Jackie Wilson headlined Freed's Brooklyn Fox labor day show, singing his latest release *You Better Know It,* which reached US # 37 and spent a week at #1 on the R&B charts. Freed's soon to follow Brooklyn Fabian-Fox Christmas show dubbed the "Christmas Jubilee of Stars," featured a bevy of teen idols along with Jackie Wilson singing his current hit *Talk That Talk,* which made it to #34 on the US pop chart and top 3 on R&B chart.

It is a well-documented fact that Jackie and Freed were friends from the Billy Ward and the Dominoes days, but the precise relationship between Freed, Jackie, Tarnopol, and Roulette remains a tantalizing mystery. We do know Nat ("The Rat") Tarnopol worked as an A&R man for Morris Levy's Roulette Records. We also know that Freed's connection with Levy started at the very dawn of the rock 'n roll era when a corporation formed by Levy, Freed and two other entities filed a copyright on the phrase "rock & roll," which Freed went on to promote and establish as a bona fide musical category. Their relationship also involved a partnership in Roulette Records in which Freed expected to receive a 50 percent share, but Levy was ruthless and was said to have never trusted someone he could not buy. Due to Freed's ever-increasing alcohol dependency, Levy felt he was too unstable and unpredictable and cast him adrift of the dealings.

Morris Levy began his career as a young hoodlum in the Bronx and graduated to shady nightclub owner. Levy attracted the interest of the FBI and the New York State Police as early as 1958 after he opened a restaurant in partnership with two known mobsters, one a convicted killer, the other an alleged captain in the Joseph Columbo crime family. Thanks to U.S. copyright law, he now stood to gain royalties every time the phrase rock and roll was used anywhere, in any context. Levy, unlike many of his contemporaries, believed rock and roll was here to stay, and would use the copyright law repeatedly over the next twenty years to acquire ownership of so many songs, and so much money, that he would later be called "The Godfather of Rock and Roll."

Nevertheless, long before that moniker attached itself to Levy, greed had become the record trade's calling card. According to Jackson, Levy was known to have said to any performer inquiring about royalties, "You want royalty? Go to England!" His attitude was, "If a guy's a cocksucker in his life, when he dies, he don't become a saint."

Freed had also come under attack after one of his shows resulted in a riot. Once the authorities looked into Freed and found his connection with Levy, the die was cast. Freed would be one of the major casualties of the payola wars. Cashbox wrote of Freed that "he suffered the most . . . for alleged wrongs that had become a way of life for many others."

Others like Nat Tarnopol.

Chapter Four

Nat "the Hero" or Nat "the Rat"

Authorities in the music and record industry and the people who knew Jackie and have written or been asked about his life, greatly differ on their opinions of Nat Tarnopol. This dichotomy of opinion is just another tantalizing example of the duality that would characterize most aspects of Jackie's personal and professional life.

None other than Ed Sullivan had this to say about the Nat and Jackie "team," excerpted from a letter on the cover of the album *Jackie Wilson at the Copa,* Brunswick label BL 54108: "It happened in 1957 in Detroit. Young Nat Tarnopol, twenty-six years old, set himself up as a theatrical agent, in a one-room office on Woodward Street. The office was not very elaborate. It cost $12 a month, $3 a week!

"On this particular afternoon, Tarnopol was awaiting an appointment with a twenty-two-year-old singer, Jackie Wilson, who had sung the lead with "The Dominoes" but had dropped out of that combination to go on his own. Tarnopol asked the young Wilson to sing a song for him and Jackie sang *Danny Boy*. That was the start of a spectacular recording combination. In five years, this two-youngster team has come up with seven Gold Records starting with *To Be Loved*, and proceeding through *Lonely Teardrops, That's Why, All My Love, Night, Doggin' Around*, and *A Woman, A Lover, A Friend*.

"I describe Tarnopol and Wilson as a team because they're bound together by a very impressive degree of loyalty, founded on deep trust in each other. And, there is an additional quality: Tarnopol is a big-time operator. He spends money generously if there is the slightest chance that it will help Jackie Wilson's career."

Sullivan later describes Tarnopol as his "young friend" so there may be some bias in his description. Also, the fact that his writing appeared on the album cover of a Tarnopol-owned Brunswick record may permit some skepticism. But he was not the only insider to take the view of Nat and Jackie as a matched set. In her autobiography, Raynoma Gordy Singleton echoes Sullivan's portrayal of Jackie and Nat as a team. "I'd become well acquainted with both Jackie and Nat Tarnopol, who always cruised through our place in tandem. Nat was the silent controlling shadow to Jackie's flashy, overpowering, 'I'm here!'"

But Raynoma found Tarnopol socially inept and inelegant. "I reached the breaking point with Tarnopol the day he arrived at our place alone. 'Hey,' he nodded to me, with no acknowledgment that we'd ever met before.

"'Oh, hi, Nat. Come on in.' Under other circumstances, I would have said that Nat was good-looking. A tall, slender white man in his mid-twenties, he was young for the success he was attaining. How was it, I wondered, that Nat could spend so much money on his apparently costly suits and still look tacky?"

Nat was either lacking in social graces or he was just simply rude. His attitude that writers were expendable and his continued snubbing of Raynoma, who had great influence on Berry Gordy and eventually Motown, were leading factors in Gordy's decision to pull away from Jackie and Tarnopol to go out on his own.

In an article entitled "Jackie Wilson: Lonely Teardrops and Endless Tragedy," published in **Sepia** magazine, Al Duckett claims: "Everyone who knows anything about the Wilson career agrees that Tarnopol and Wilson made each other. Nat guided Jackie to stardom and the impact of the Wilson career took Nat to the heights of his own business."

Duckett also calls Tarnopol, "The mastermind behind Jackie Wilson's meteoritic rise during the rock and roll era of the early sixties. From the beginning, back in Detroit, where Jackie, a twenty-three-year-old unknown, walked into his office to audition, Tarnopol took him under his wing."

Tarnopol may have been rude, tacky, and who knows what else, but he was not stupid. Duckett quoted Tarnopol in **Sepia** magazine as having said, "I flipped when I first heard that voice of such great versatility and operatic quality. I knew that here was an unusual talent."

We also have a few examples of Jackie's own feelings about his manager. In his interview with Norman Knight he said, "Well, actually I met Nat through Al Green, who was the manager of LaVern Baker at the time; and we were all from Detroit. Nat was a young, hotheaded kid who wanted to get ahead and he was doing all the publishing for Green. Al Green took me around after the Dominoes and he started to manage me and he got me a contract through LaVern Baker with Decca, which was for Brunswick. Then, God rest his soul, he died. Then Nat decided he was going to try his hand, although there was several other guys around, Nat just packed up one day and took me by the arm of his [sic] rain coat."

On the album cover for *You Ain't Heard Nothin' Yet,* Brunswick label BL 54100, Jackie writes about his desire to make an album of hits by his favorite artist, Al Jolson: "I never thought that this ambition would take shape this soon, but thanks to my manager, Nat Tarnopol, without whose faith and foresight I might never be writing this now, my dream has finally become a reality."

Again, this letter suffers from the stigma of having been something Tarnopol himself would have sanctioned, but with the exception of a purported falling out with Nat later in his career, Jackie remained staunchly loyal to Nat, performing when and where he was told to perform, singing what he was told to sing, and dressing and acting the way he was directed. Does this sound like the actions of a person's free will?

According to his third wife, Lynn Belle Guidry (nee Dupont, also known previously as Lynn Crochet), "Jackie trusted Nat Tarnopol implicitly and foolishly signed over power of attorney to him . . . I never liked Nat Tarnopol from the time I met him."

Musicologist Robert Pruter, who appears to have done the most research on the life of Jackie Wilson prior to this book, had this to say about Jackie's manager: "Nat Tarnopol appears to come out as the heavy in this story, but in the course of research for this article it was discovered he had defenders, notably Dick Jacobs, who, before his untimely death in 1988, spoke fondly of him.

Another defender was former Decca A&R chief Henry Jerome, who said, "Nobody ever gives credit to the manager who does all the work in getting the artist on record and into the clubs and builds his career. Nat was a really nice guy who worked hard and built Jackie Wilson's career . . ."

Tim Holmes reports in his **Musician** article that Dick Jacobs claimed Jackie chose Nat as his manager after Al Green died. "I had met Nat once very briefly while in Detroit on a disk jockey tour, when he'd showed me some songs that he'd published. In those days Nat worked as a tire salesman, but his heart was always in the record industry. Now, with the chance to oversee the burgeoning career of Jackie Wilson, Nat was in the game for real."

There is a general consensus among writers of the times and historians of music that Nat groomed Jackie's recordings and live performances to appeal to a white, middle class audience. He booked Jackie in many of the major entertainment centers in Hollywood, Las Vegas, New York, and Miami. In his book **Soul Music A-Z**, Hugh Gregory wrote: "Throughout the early 1960s Tarnopol guided Jackie's career toward the glitz of Vegas and Hollywood. The results were extraordinary (and heartbreaking)." He goes on to list Jackie's many hits but does not explain his "heartbreaking" comment.

Lee Hildebrand, author of **Stars of Soul** and **Rhythm & Blues,** concluded: "Wilson maintained a strong chart presence through 1960, hitting #1 R&B with *You Better Know It, Doggin' Around,* and *A Woman, A Lover, A Friend.* Tarnopol then began grooming him as a middle-of-the-road crooner, and the singer's material became increasingly conservative."

Jackie had his second million seller, *Night*, which hit US #4. *Night* is an operatic ballad set to the melody of *My Heart at Thy Sweet Voice* from Camille Saint-Seans' ***"Samson and Delilah.***" Jackie also made a hit of *(You Were Made For) All My Love* (US #12). *Alone at Last,* based on the melody of *Tchaikovsky's Piano Concerto #1 in B flat*, reached Pop #8. In December, Jackie was voted *Entertainer of the Year* by ***Cashbox*** magazine.

What many writers fail to take into account was that Jackie Wilson was a formidable talent, perhaps too talented a performer for the brash, unpolished Tarnopol to handle. He cast Jackie about like a fly fisherman after a prize bass, from rhythm and blues to soul to rock, from nightclubs to records to concerts—but without a firm plan, a stable identity, an identified audience which Jackie could cultivate and make his own. Because of (or perhaps in spite of) his incredible range and versatility, Jackie was almost able to adapt to whatever pond Tarnopol cast him into. Jackie spent the sixties bouncing from soul to pop, scoring only six Top Ten rhythm and blues hits during the decade, compared to his ten Top Tens between 1958 and 1960. Had Jackie's global talent been honed, directed, and nurtured by someone equally talented in management, Jackie might have crossed the racial barrier and become the kind of phenomenon Elvis Presley became, during the time in question.

It's thirty years too late for "if onlys," but had Jackie been planted in the Motown garden of stars, or been fortunate enough to have a Colonel Tom Parker on his team, he might have received the recognition his tremendous talent deserved. Robert Pruter opined that it was one of Jackie's great misfortunes that he was not able to spend more time in association with Gordy. "Had the singer been brought into Gordy's creative stable at Motown instead of being kept in servitude at Brunswick Records for his entire eighteen-year solo career, he might have been spared the schlock that marred much of his post-Gordy output."

Part of the problem was that Tarnopol steered Jackie toward the supper club set with pop standards and a watered-down version of his virtuosity because Tarnopol felt rock 'n roll and rhythm and blues were passing fads, and that most of the records would be purchased by the "white bread well-to-do" instead of teenagers both black and white. In hindsight we now know Tarnopol was dead wrong.

And what did Jackie think about all this? In the liner notes for an Ace Records re-release of *Reet Petite* in 1984, Bill Millar quotes Jackie from an interview with Bob Fisher: "I found it difficult to adjust, very much so. All of a sudden black was black and white was white, and each wanted to perform his own music. For someone like me who had been used to both audiences it was an insult to record one thing and not the other. It left me quite shattered."

It was not just Tarnopol's bad judgment of public demand that caused Jackie to waver at the peak of his career. It was also the fact that it was the record industry's standard operating procedure to take advantage of black entertainers. Author Gary Herman, writing in **Rock 'n Roll Babylon**, discusses what it meant to a musician in the midst of desegregation: "Unfortunately, the desegregation of music and audiences made little difference to the practice of exploiting performers. White and black alike were ripped off, because any inexperienced performer with an inadequate understanding of the business and inadequate advisors was a potential target for bad (or no) royalty deals, shark-like managers and agents, diabolical contracts and Faustian agreements. If blacks suffered more from this institutional cheating, it was because they tended to have less experience of business, less effective representation and perhaps even a lower level of aspiration. On top of that, the 'race' market was smaller and poorer than the white market, which meant that deals were usually worse and the ultimate rewards invariably smaller.

"If there was no specific move against racism or for black equality in the early days of rock 'n roll, there was a great deal of feeling that blacks should, at least, assert themselves and protect their own interests. The sixties consequently saw the growth of independent black record labels, song publishers, agencies and managements, and the prime example of this was Berry Gordy's Motown Company."

Not all black performers were as docile as Jackie. **In Nowhere to Run: The Story of Soul Music** by Gerri Hirshey, Hugo Peritti, a producer at RCA, related how Sam Cooke would get around his indentured servitude with the William Morris Agency.

"'Sam would disappear,' Hugo says. 'No one knew where he was. What he'd do is this: He'd go on the road . . . he and a band and a few guys would just go down south and hit a little town, say Wheeling, West Virginia. And he'd go to the local promoter and say, 'Tomorrow night we're going to give a concert and dance. 'They'd put up banners and all that, and Sam would do the gig. He made all cash, put the money in his pocket, and left. Then he'd hit another town. You could never pin him down. He moved so fast there was no way to prove he was doing it. Maybe taking those secret trips helped settle him down. You know, he felt that he was always giving so much to agents. He'd say, 'I want to make some money for myself.' A few days out there, and he'd put a roll in his pocket all right. It may not have been what he'd earn in a night at the Copa, but I guess it was worth more in peace of mind."

There is no evidence Jackie ever dared such a brazen act. In his book **The Death of Rhythm & Blues**, Nelson George makes an insightful comparison of Jackie and Sam Cooke. Both were athletic, handsome, with passionate voices and great sex appeal. In fact, they were great friends and shared much in common, including the love of their country and music. In the early 1960s, George claims, the two stars were on equal footing in the realm of rhythm and blues, but Cooke would go on to make a greater contribution and have significant influence on black music. He writes: "Cooke was a marching black, and Wilson was not. Wilson's career in fact illustrated the worst scenario a singular and instinctive black vocalist could face, while Cooke would embody the ambitions of his people and the contradictory ways those ambitions were often satisfied. Wilson was strangled by the status quo; Cooke, a trailblazing businessman and a mass-market commodity, was a vision of the good-and bad of black music's future."

George calls Jackie "Tarnopol's cash cow" and complains "he received none of the innovative and sensitive guidance his talent deserved." During the sixties, when black awareness was at its peak, George wonders why Jackie did not demand more control over his own career. The answer is as simple as it is horrific, and there is not a note of sensitivity in it.

Robert Pruter in his *Goldmine* article on Jackie, recalls a scene from the Robert Townsend film *The Five Heartbeats*. " . . . a particularly melodramatic moment takes place when a record company executive and his henchmen rough up a recalcitrant singer and then hang him by his feet out of a hotel window to force him to sign a contract. Insiders in the record biz know the scene is a reference to the great Jackie Wilson, perhaps the most tragic figure in the history of rhythm 'n blues." The window hanging incident was confirmed by Jackie's songwriting cousin, Billy Davis, who felt it might have happened more than once. Davis described coming back to Jackie's apartment in the Alvin Hotel to find Jackie "white as a ghost." After a long discussion, Jackie told Davis what happened. Jackie was horrified his mother would find out and made Davis swear not to tell anyone so she would not. "Jackie had a number of companies who wanted to record him over the years," said Davis, "but he never went to them because of fear."

In **Chicago Soul**, Pruter claims Sonny Woods, a vocalist with the Midnighters, corroborates the incident, that it took place in 1964 and coincided with the renewal of Jackie's Brunswick contract, expiring at that time. Decca gave half the Brunswick label to Tarnopol for making sure Jackie renewed it. By 1966 Brunswick had only one artist—Jackie Wilson—and by 1970 Tarnopol had made enough money off his "cash cow" to purchase the remaining half of Brunswick.

In his interview with Ted Fox, Bob Thiele recalled, "He [Tarnopol] even wound up at Brunswick because Decca—after I had left the company—in an attempt to keep Jackie Wilson, gave him the label. They gave him Brunswick; that was part of the deal."

Unlike Tarnopol, Brunswick was no upstart. It had been around since 1916 and had contracts with major stars Arturo Toscanini, Bing Crosby, and Fred Astaire, as well as Al Jolson, Jackie's childhood idol, whose first big hits, *Sonny Boy* and *There's a Rainbow Round My Shoulder,* appeared in his second film ***The Singing Fool*** in 1928. Brunswick also made Rudolph Valentino's first and only recording, but it was so awful it was never released.

The label underwent several transformations while handling the

Mills Brothers, the Andrews Sisters, and Harry James, then it was closed down for a time, and finally sold to Decca in 1942. Decca reopened it 1957 during the time period Jackie, the Chi-Lites and the Crickets were its primary stars. Despite this lineup of talent, Brunswick executives would eventually refer to their company as "the house that Jackie Wilson built."

Several writers have noted that despite Brunswick's dubious reputation, its creative staff is nevertheless respected simply for the quality and quantity of the music they brought to the world over the years. All Tarnopol really had going for him was Jackie Wilson, and he was doing quite well financially because of it. Some of the money that should have found its way into Jackie's pocket— but didn't—went to grease the palms of disk jockeys in a trade for generous air time for Brunswick's records. Perhaps this is what Ed Sullivan meant when he wrote: "Tarnopol is a big-time operator. He spends money generously if there is the slightest chance that it will help Jackie Wilson's career."

Bill Pollack reports in an August 14, 1978, **Village Voice** article entitled "Jackie Wilson's Lonely Tears: The Medical, Legal, and Financial Tragedy of Mr. Soul," that Tarnopol and six other Brunswick executives were indicted in a payola scandal in June 1975. Pollack claims in the article, "They were charged with conspiring to sell records to distributors for cash or merchandise, then using the cash for payoffs to disk jockeys and radio-station program directors." "According to the indictment, since these cash sales were not entered in the company books, the officials were guilty of tax evasion and of defrauding their own artists.

Fredric Dannen, in his book **Hit Men**, added some detail to Pollack's account. Dannen claims the Brunswick executives' indictment included a charge of taking $343,000 in kickbacks from retailers to whom they sold records below wholesale.

In February 1976, a Newark jury convicted Tarnopol of one count of conspiracy and 38 counts of mail fraud (Pollack claims 22 counts). Carl Davis and Melvin Moore, Brunswick's director of national programs, were found innocent due to their lack of direct knowledge of what was going on in the New York offices. However, despite defense protestations that selling records at a discount was common business practice and a marketing necessity for a small company competing in the trenches with major record producers, three other Brunswick executives were convicted along with Tarnopol based partially on the testimony of Eugene Record, leader of Brunswick's most successful act in the 1970s, the Chi-Lites. Records told the jury how he had been threatened and assaulted by Tarnopol's "associates" over a royalty dispute. The following April, Judge Frederick Lacey sentenced Tarnopol to three years in prison and ordered him to pay a fine of $10,000.

Nat did not earn the moniker "The Rat" for nothing. He appealed his conviction to the United States Third Circuit Court of Appeals. It was overturned, and he was granted a second trial in November 1977. The trial began the following May, but ended in a mistrial when the government's case failed for lack of a Brunswick artist who would now testify on the witness stand he or she was defrauded.

Dannen wrote: "The loss was a sad blow because Tarnopol was a notorious abuser of artists, on par with Morris Levy. He had taken ruthless advantage of Jackie Wilson by designing contracts that left the singer perpetually in debt to Brunswick, even as his records made hundreds of thousands for the label. The writing credit for Wilson's *Doggin' Around* was listed to Paul Tarnopol, Nat's son, who wasn't born when the song was recorded (and who now runs Brunswick). Even the appellate judge who overturned Tarnopol's conviction took pains to note in his decision that 'there was evidence from which a jury could find that artists were defrauded of royalties.'"

People who knew Jackie in his boxing days were aware of his mother's dislike for the sport because of its reputation as a gangster business. Because of his friendship with Smokey Robinson and Aretha Franklin, Reverend Dr. Anthony Campbell knew something about the inner workings of the business. "Well, the music business was a gangster business. Let's be frank about it. Berry Gordy in his biography talks about the trouble he had getting paid when he made a record distribution deal. The reason that he ended up owning his own songs was—I think to the detriment of his artists whom he in effect, well, not cheated, but he took advantage of the naivete of our copyright laws—he was trying to protect the fact that when a black artist did a piece of music it was easily stolen. By the time you sued everybody in sight, you could not collect any money. And it was not uncommon for people to have million-record sellers and not get a dime in royalties . . . and besides in the city of Detroit, it was the numbers bankers and the extortionists and the boosters who had money to invest in record companies. I mean, you couldn't go down to the bank and [apply] for a small business loan. You'd never get it."

When asked by an interviewer why he never left Brunswick, Jackie replied enigmatically, "My mind would say go but my soul would say stay." Given that Jackie did whatever he could to keep the details of his subjugation by Brunswick a secret from his mother, it is strange that she should have remained totally unaware of the music industry's criminal misconduct. Regardless, when she forced Jackie out of the boxing ring, she inadvertently tossed him into the fire.

Chapter Five

The Second Bang
A Woman, A Lover, A Friend

The Apollo Theater in Harlem was the stage on which soul music was born and bred. James Brown, Sam Cooke, Ray Charles, and Jackie Wilson were the early soul stars because their songs reflected the soul of the black community, living within the circle of the Apollo's shadow. Black pride was blossoming in the sixties, and soul was the first true musical form that gave celebrity and dignity to being black. It was not aimed at white audiences and with exception of some notable attempts by such artists as Van Morrison, Tom Jones, and the Righteous Brothers, whose sound was labeled "blue-eyed soul" by Georgie Woods, a disk jockey at station WDAS in Philadelphia, white performers were never able to successfully produce music that conveyed emotions only blacks could feel.

Born of gospel, soul was music with a message. While rhythm and blues reflected the frustrations of ghetto life, soul was full of optimism intended for better, more equal, and loving times. According to Apollo Theater historian Ted Fox, Jackie Wilson helped define the sound and feel of soul. In **Showtime at the Apollo,** he writes, "He could get down and slug out a rocking tune, but he also polished his act and style with a different kind of pop sensibility... In May 1963, Jackie Wilson became the Apollo's all-time box-office champ until James Brown set another record the following year." James Brown had one of the hottest bands in the country—the famous Flames—something Jackie was never fortunate enough to have.

The Encyclopedia of Rock and Roll says of Jackie, "With an output ranging from quasi-operatic ballads to gritty, belting dance favorites, Jackie Wilson was a supreme rhythm and blues vocal stylist who helped pave the way for the soul music explosion of the sixties yet never quite became part of it." On April 28, 1962, **the** *Amsterdam News* published the following news report, headlined: *Jackie Hits Bigtime at Copacabana.*

Open:

When Jackie opened his show at the Copacabana on April 28, 1962, he was only really known well from his one-man appearances at the Apollo. His Copa performance was something else entirely. Accompanied by a conductor, two guitarists, a piano player, three violinists, and a backup vocal group, Jackie entered the world of pop and the Copa's glamorous crowd approved.

Critics began calling him "electric," "sensational," and "a young Billy Daniels."

Billy Daniels was known for his strong vocal and visual style. While *Amsterdam News* admitted Jackie had the fire and verve, they also asserted he was most definitely "not a Billy Daniels" and that his range, depth, and flexibility still needed some polish. In fact, Jackie's Copa booking was really a fluke. Another performer backed out of his contract at the last moment. Copa owner Jules Podell signed Jackie without an audition and crossed his fingers. Podell was so impressed he ultimately signed Jackie to a three-year contract.

Jackie Wilson was known as Mr. Excitement from his days at the Apollo because he packed the kind of wallop in his first song that most performers save for last. But in his personal life, Jackie might just as well have been known as Mr. Enigma. There were two Jackie Wilsons—the yin and the yang, the black and the white, the real and imagined, the good and the bad. The more fame and adoration he achieved, the more dual his personality became, and each person who knew him saw someone different.

Born into the sign of Gemini on June 9, 1934, Jackie Wilson led two lives. One was as a husband and father, married to Freda Wilson, a longtime sweetheart. Together, Freda and Jackie had four children: Jackie Denice, Sandra Kay, Jackie, Jr., and Anthony Duane. By contrast, the other Jackie was a man on the move, on the road and on the way up, with hot and cold running women, one of whom he married at the same time he was married to Freda.

As reported in a **Jet** magazine article entitled "It's Tough to Be the Wife of A Star," Freda accepted that Jackie was on the road a great part of the year, but took comfort from the fact that he re- turned to their fourteen room Highland Park apartment for holi- days. She felt Jackie was the "world's greatest father" and that his kids had great respect and admiration for their famous dad.

Freda claims not to have been upset by all the publicity regard- ing the many women Jackie knew. She was confident in Jackie's loyalty because their relationship went back to high school— that Jackie was her only boyfriend and that their love had grown strong over the years. Her role in life was as a mother and that role re- quired confidence and understanding in Jackie's long absences, as well as in the way in which he made his living.

Freda had no interest in traveling with Jackie or sharing his fame. Interviews with Jackie's various associates, valets, and others con- firm she stayed completely in the background. She received calls from time to time from people with gossip about Jackie's extra- marital love life. Yet after she slammed the phone down a few times, they finally stopped calling.

Over the ten years of their marriage Freda learned to adapt to the periods of loneliness by focusing attention on her children's needs, knowing that when Jackie tired of life in the spotlight, he would return home, and they would live like a regular married couple. She had accepted the fact that Jackie was popular since the time he'd won his first talent contest and was already getting re- quests for autographs. He told her: "Don't worry, honey, my first love is you always."

Jackie met Harlean Harris in 1953 at around the time he replaced

Clyde McPhatter in the Dominoes. Harlean was fourteen years old and president of the 25-member Billy Ward and the Dominoes fan club. A staunch McPhatter fan, she was quickly won over by his replacement when she saw Jackie perform the first time at the Apollo Theater in Harlem. Al Duckett writing in the April 1979 issue of *Sepia* quoted Harlean, "He was multi-talented. I have seen him bring the crowd at the Apollo Theater to its feet. I have watched as he did the same thing at the downtown theaters. At the swank Copacabana in New York, he won a standing ovation and such a great reception that Jules Podell, the boss of the Copa, signed him to a three-year contract."

It also amazed her that Jackie never took voice lessons and could not read music: "But he had an ear," Duckett said. "And if he heard it, he could sing it."

Harlean became a model some time after their first meeting. They dated from 1958 through 1962. At some point in time she also dated Sam Cooke. Jackie saw her photo on a magazine cover and sought to congratulate her shortly after he'd left the Dominoes and gone solo. She went to see him at the Apollo, met him back-stage, and their love affair was ignited. They had a son named John Dominick, whom they nicknamed Petie.

According to Lynn Guidry, in March 1967 Jackie and his friend, Jimmy Smith, were caught with two twenty-four-year-old white women in their motel in South Carolina and were arrested on a morals charge. Details of the incident were well publicized, and Tarnopol decided Jackie needed to clean up his image. Tarnopol arranged a quick wedding for Jackie and Harlean Harris. Jackie paid a minimal fine, and the whole incident soon blew over, at least as far as the public was concerned.

Privately, however, the Gemini aspect of Jackie's life continued to play itself out. He wasn't just a family man, he was a two-family man. One could claim there was a spiral of immorality beginning to swirl around him. You could not whip women into a frenzy night after night in city upon city and not have some fallout drop on you.

In an interview with Arnold Shaw recorded in **Honkers and Shouters**: **The Golden Years of Rhythm & Blues**, Jackie recalled: "Nineteen sixty was the year we had a problem in New Orleans. At this theater, the girls were getting excited and jumping up on the stage. I didn't mind, but the police did. They started pushing the girls around—to get them off the stage. They were rough. And so I shoved a cop. The next thing you know, they arrested me for assaulting an officer."

From **Nowhere to Run:** "It was the live act, more than the records, however, that made Jackie Wilson a dyed-in-the-mohair soul man. An ex-prizefighter with the heart of a lion or a fool, he would willingly leap into a sea of female arms that tore the clothes from him and raked at his flesh. In New Orleans in 1961, diving into the frenzy he had caused got him arrested when he shoved a cop who was roughing up swooning women.

"In black clubs he had the icy effrontery to come at them with *Danny Boy* and wail away at it until they banged the tables and screamed. Jackie Wilson was well aware of his dangerous potency.

And, still, he pushed it.

"Between Jackie Wilson's sets, stage hands sopped up pools of sweat . . . He threw himself around without regard for his safety or his wardrobe. Besides having dirty knees, the fancy stage clothes were soaked in funky brine. Many suits he could wear only once. Taking the stage at the outset, he was icy-cool devastation in a boxy silk suit and spectator shoes. Leaving it, he looked like a man who had walked ten miles in a driving rain storm.

"It followed that female hysteria popped and crackled danger-ously around him wherever he went. One night, in a New York hotel room, a woman brought to the edge pumped bullets into the cause of her madness, and Jackie Wilson nearly died. It happened in 1961, the best year of his career, in which he had six bestsellers."

Jackie attempted to view life with humor whenever possible. Once when asked by the chaperone of the Supremes if he could look after them while she went to lunch, Jackie responded with a grin, "Oh, sure, I'll watch them little girls like a hawk!"

Dick Jacobs told Tim Holmes that Jackie loved the sound of sustained strings behind his voice and would say, "Dick, gimme them substained strings." Jacobs never knew if Jackie pronounced it incorrectly on purpose or not, but it became a big joke among the group of musicians.

Jackie's occasional bouts of humor did not shield him from the inevitable. His personal and professional life came crashing down around his ears the night he was shot. There were several versions of the story—the actual story as told by his close associates many years later, and the sanitized ones that appeared in the media in order to hide the fact Jackie was one party of a love quadrangle made up of Freda, Harlean, and a twenty-eight-year-old woman named Juanita Jones.

The public story, as recorded by Major Robinson in his **Jet** magazine article "Rock *'n* Roll Idol Jackie Wilson Felled by Fan's Gun," went like this: "On Valentine's Day in the early morning hours of February 15, 1961, Jackie was returning to his sixth floor apartment at 408 West 57th Street in New York, after a late show at 3:00 a.m. He saw Juanita sitting in the hallway but ignored her. He went into his apartment and a few minutes later, he heard a knock at the door. According to Robinson, Jackie 'denied her an audience' and started to shut the door. When Jones pulled out a .38 caliber revolver from the waist of her pants, aimed it at her head, and threatened to end it all, Jackie lunged for the gun and was shot in the stomach and thigh during the struggle.

"Jackie limped down to the street where a passing patrolman, Donald Roberts, found him and rushed him to Roosevelt Hospital. One bullet was removed in a two-hour operation, the second remained in his body. Jackie was still listed in critical condition when Juanita Jones was arraigned in felony court. She was paroled on $2,500 and ordered to appear for a hearing on February 28th. Some news reports state Jackie was given last Rites."

The media portrayed Jones as a stalker. Neighbors said she was quiet, moody, and played Jackie Wilson records constantly. Jackie's associates reported she was always hanging around backstage near his dressing room whenever he was in New York, and that this was not the first incident of her "shadowing" Jackie. According to a reporter for the *New York Times*, Jackie told the police Jones had been annoying him with phone calls.

To the police, the former WAC admitted she fell in love with Jackie when she first heard him sing *Lonely Teardrops* three years earlier—that she was "mixed up" and certainly did not mean to hurt Jackie. She sobbed hysterically while in the precinct station, professing her love for him.

In an interesting side-note to the piece, Robinson claims Jackie "grosses more than $350,000 yearly" and that Nat Tarnopol, whom Jackie regards as a brother, was "near collapse."

When Jackie was shot, Freda rushed to New York along with Jackie's mother Eliza Wilson and his sister, Joyce Lee. The hospital received thousands of phone calls from people conveying their well-wishes and requesting information on his condition. One hospital worker was reported as saying the staff had never experienced anything like it. In the **Jet** article about her life with Jackie, Freda praised the hospital staff for helping her answer the 10,000 letters and telegrams sent by Jackie's fans.

Though the shooting incident was well-covered, most of the coverage was incidental, such as the small story hidden on page 26 of the **New York Post** on the day after the shooting. One wonders what kind of coverage Elvis would have received had he been shot in a similar manner.

In his interview with Norman Knight, Jackie implicitly confirmed some aspects of the media's account. "I was shot in the stomach. Well, I still have the bullet. I still carry it. It's in my back but it's in a safe place, just can't move it because it hasn't moved . . . we didn't prosecute her, she wasn't shooting at me, she was going to shoot herself. When the person's a little off at the time, they're kind of strong. I grabbed the pistol but I am the one who got shot." Jackie either failed or chose not to mention he lost a kidney as a result of the shooting.

In the **Honkers and Shouters** interview Jackie reduced the incident to a few sentences, calling Jones "some crazy chick," and showed he still did not appreciate the subtlety of cause and effect: "We also had some trouble in 1961. That was when some crazy chick took a shot at me and nearly put me away for good. It took some time, some good doctors, and a lot of help from the 'Man Upstairs' before I got out of the hospital and back to where I could perform.

"But do you know? In both those years, 1960-61, my records were hitting the charts as if nothing happened. I had five bestsellers in '60 and six in '61."

Robert Pruter reported a slightly different version which rings truer and is a more likely scenario. "The impassioned hysteria Wilson generated rebounded against him in February 1961, when he was shot by a "fatal attraction" fan in a jealous rage. His model girlfriend, Harlean Harris, in a visit to his New York apartment, was being attacked by the fan and Wilson intervened to take two slugs, one in the abdomen and one in the buttocks. The shooting left him in critical condition and he was bedridden for a month. Contemporary accounts omitted all mention of Ms. Harris as Wilson was married at the time, to Freda [sic] Hall Wilson. Wilson's personal life became increasingly messy after this incident. In 1964, Freda, who had been his wife for fourteen years, filed for a divorce, and thereafter there were constant hassles over support payments for her and their four children."

Bill Frazier, Jackie's valet at the time he was shot, gives a slightly different account. Frazier and Jackie's driver and road manager, J. J. Newberry, dropped Jackie and Harlean off at the West 57th Street apartment after the couple had seen a movie. Jackie's apartment door was adjacent to the stairway and Juanita Jones was waiting for him there. Jackie told Harlean to go inside the apartment and she had done so when the shooting took place.

Frazier, who worked for Hank Ballard and the Midnighters prior to working for Jackie, claims Jones and Jackie had been lovers for a long time and Jackie visited her in her Seventh Avenue apartment from time to time. "That was if he didn't have a date or something he'd feel like . . . well, he want to go there and we get the limousine, the car and go upstairs, take care of the number and then come on back down. You know, what I'm talking about?" When Jackie spurned her for reasons unknown, she retaliated. Although we know the reason Jones was angry, we are left wondering if suicide was really her intent.

While Jackie was recuperating in Roosevelt Hospital, Frazier recalled, "I couldn't go see him because at that time I would always keep his drugs or whatever. They didn't allow me to go near him."

Jackie was taking pain killers by prescription when he could get them from a doctor, or from "his girls" when he couldn't. Frazier also revealed that Jackie was "messed up" financially after the shooting and that Morris Levy sent a man by the name of Johnny Roberts ". . . to keep hooks on Jackie because he'd been messing up cocaine and, you know what I'm talking 'bout. In other words, keep all the riff-raff away. And that's how Johnny Roberts got in."

Bill Murry describes Johnny Roberts as "one of those gangsters that used to come on the road. A little Italian-looking guy with black hair and coal black eyes to match. Johnny represented the people who were into Nat Tarnopol. Johnny was out there on the road, always in eyesight, to make sure Jackie didn't f _ _ _ up and to protect their interests." Johnny's view of his job description included counting every penny Jackie earned and spent.

Johnny Roberts was, in fact, a mob enforcer. His boss was a man named Gaetano "Tommy" Vastola. Vastola was a part owner of the Queens Booking Agency, which acted as Jackie's booking agent, as well as many other black artists during that time. Vastola also controlled Nat. According to Dannen in **Hit Men**, "Vastola was the nephew of Dominick Ciaffone, a.k.a. Swats Mulligan, who was a soldier for the Genovese crime family. Vastola had several nicknames: "Corky," "the Big Guy," and "the Galoot." Vastola was an associate of Morris Levy for more than thirty years and was convicted with him in 1989. A federal wiretap recorded the proud words of uncle Swats about his nephew: "This kid could tear a human being apart with his hands."

The Galoot pseudonym for Vastola was accurate. He was a brutish man with no musical talent or knowledge save his long association with Levy. His job to keep tabs on Alan Freed in the mid-fifties brought him into the business. Vastola owned a recording studio called City Lights, managed the Cleftones, and had some interest in Frankie Lymon and the Teenagers. He was also part-owner of Queens Booking Agency. When members of Vastola's organization became involved in drugs and gambling, the FBI obtained the court's permission to wire tap him, thus bringing all his operations into the open, including an illegal sale of five million cut out records and tapes to Philadelphia wholesaler John LaMonte. There was some disagreement among the parties, however, as to the quality of the merchandise, and LaMonte refused to pay for the shipment. Vastola simply broke his face. Having served two prior jail sentences for extortion, Vastola admitted on tape, "We're gonna wind up in the joint."

Like Elvis, Jackie had his own entourage with him at all times. Perhaps because the faces changed from time to time, they never acquired a descriptive name like the Memphis Mafia. Prior to Johnny Roberts' arrival on the scene, Jackie's road manager was August Sims. Sims typified the bodyguard stereotype. A former fighter, he weighed 230 pounds and had been the masseur and bodyguard for Sugar Ray Robinson for over a decade prior to coming into Jackie's employ. Sims provided protection for Jackie, as well as ensuring that Jackie showed up for his gigs and that the money he made found its way to Brunswick's New York office.

About Sims, Lamar Cochran recalled, "We used to go up and get our hair fixed because we used to wear the do as you call it, the processing thing. . . . Sims got Danny "Bang-Bang" Womble to travel with us to fix his hair so Jackie would have his own barber and hair stylist with him . . . Sims traveled. Sims would go down to Philadelphia and buy his [Jackie's] clothes or have his clothes made, and in the meantime have him something made as well. . . . Nat Tarnopol and them give him that kind of clutch, and he was handling the ends as far as the money concerns and so forth, and he kinda turned out to be the road manager and the hotel booker . . . Jackie had quite a few people out there with him. The entourage used to be like two in the car, myself, and another driver, an extra driver, but he almost didn't believe no son of a bitch could drive no longer than me, other than [Clarence] Watley because we knew the bumps in the road and the short cuts."

Despite Jackie's assertion that his recordings continued hitting the charts after the shooting, many music historians and others who have written about him have proffered the opinion Jackie was never quite the same afterward. It was as if the incident itself, or some resulting aftershock, took the wind out of his sails and destroyed the spark within him. Perhaps he met with the sad realization that fame and infinite women were not all they were cracked up to be. Either Jackie was already on the road to bad times before the Jones incident brought him to his senses, or his frenetic lifestyle was simply beginning to catch up with him . . . or both. The shot was just a precipitating factor that added fuel to the fire.

Despite Freda's statement to Major Robinson in **Jet**: "When I answered, 'I do,' I meant it, and nothing will ever shatter the dream house that Jackie and I live in," she was finally forced to face the truth about the father of her four children when the IRS seized her home for unpaid taxes.

Freda was caught totally unaware by this action. It was her understanding Tarnopol took care of the taxes on Jackie's $263,000 salary. Freda had no idea Jackie was broke, but he somehow managed to make arrangements with the IRS to buy his home back at an auction. Tired of Jackie's notorious philandering, Freda finally filed for divorce after thirteen years of marriage. The divorce was granted in 1965. Freda retained their house and was granted a $10,000 lump sum and $200 per week child support.

Although there is no evidence of it, there must have been a confrontation in the hospital between Harlean and Freda Wilson. Perhaps the time spent fighting for his life in a hospital room made Jackie think hard about his life. It could have been any number of events occurring in his private or professional life that somehow escaped the prying eyes of the media. Nonetheless, while the nature of his thinking is unknown, the path his life took from that point is well-documented. His Gemini duality seemed to grow with each club date and chart hit. While Jackie may have tamed his stage act, he made up for it by living life in a faster lane, and in so doing, wandered off the highway of success and was lost.

People who knew Jackie the longest were the ones who could best see the difference in him. Bill Murry , who emceed on the road with Jackie for many years, got to know him at a football game in Detroit in 1953 when Jackie jokingly tried to steal his hat. Murry was in show business for many years and is often confused with actor Bill Murray of television's *Saturday Night Live* fame. (Bill Murray also stared in the movie *Ghostbusters* and *Ghostbusters II*. In fact, the latter, released in 1989, featured one of Jackie's Wilson's biggest hits, *Higher and Higher,* which played a pivotal role in the movie's plot. Two versions of the song were used: the original by Jackie and a sound-alike rendition done by Howard Huntsberry. Ironically, Huntsberry also played the part of Jackie Wilson in the 1987 movie *La Bamba*, which was about the life of Ritchie Valens.) Jackie's music has been used in several movies, including the title theme song sung during the opening credits of Kirk Douglas's 1968 movie, *A Lovely Way to Die*. Murry recalls, "Before Jackie got shot, he was a much better performer. James Brown couldn't touch Jackie before he was shot, but he slowed down and changed his routine after."

In his autobiography, **James Brown: The Godfather of Soul**, Brown has this to say about Jackie's post-shooting persona: "[Sometime around 1966] I saw them (the Jacksons) again, in Chicago, when I was playing the Regal. By that time I wasn't playing the theaters any more except for the Regal and the Apollo. I think Al Green was on the show, and Jackie Wilson, too. Jackie had gotten wild and crazy after being shot—he was drinking a lot and using drugs pretty heavy. They had to lock him in the dressing room and make him stay there until he got straight, then he came out and did a great show. But it was terrible to see Jackie in such bad shape."

Jones was not the only angry woman to retaliate against Jackie. According to Jackie's favorite emcee, Odell "Gorgeous" George: " . . . He (Jackie) got in trouble with the law a lot of times. One time in St. Louis, Missouri some lady said that Jackie Wilson was the father of her kid and the sheriff had a warrant out for Jackie. It was during The Battle of the Stars. Jackie was in it, Sam Cooke, B.B. King, Chuck Jackson, Patti LaBelle and the Bluebells, (and) the Drifters. There were a lot of acts on this show. And we was on stage and what happened was the sheriff was getting ready to take him into jail and I said 'Man, you can't do it.' He said, 'We don't want to do this, but we're just doing our duty.' Well, the promoter said why don't you just let him do a show, man, and he'll go with you, and Jackie agreed to go with him. Dig this. So Jackie was on the stage and part of . . . that boxing thing he was doing it on stage, boom, bomp, bomp, *Lonely Teardrops*. He would jump and box and jump and do the James Cagney and box and he jumped and then everybody decided to go on the stage so Jackie could escape like a finale. Sam Cooke, Jackie Wilson, me, everybody was on stage, like ten acts and we were dancing. And the police was talking, the sheriff was talking, they was back there somewhere and we went and opened a bathroom window. The driver and the valet took Jackie's clothes and the bodyguard and put them in his car and put the car right on the side of the bathroom window and opened up the top, the windshield, you know the top of the car, and opened it up. . . Jackie Wilson boxed and boxed and we blocked the aisle and he ran to his dressing room, jumped out the window and jumped into the car and disappeared."

Jackie was known to throw violent temper tantrums on a regular basis. He often got into fist fights with his road manager, Sims, though they usually ended with hugging and laughter. Jackie boxing was a common sight, according to George, because Jackie idolized James Cagney. "He used to often tell me he would like to do some movies. Jackie wanted to be a gangster, though, but he wasn't the type. He didn't do any movies, though, because he was always booked. . . in them days he was under pressure. I mean, here's a cat used to sing every night of the week in different locations." One of Jackie's performance mannerisms, hitching his pants up with his forearms, was a direct take on Cagney's inimitable style.

Joseph Redding, a cousin of the late singer Otis Redding, recalled an incident of Jackie's temper. "The Duval County Armory in Jacksonville (Florida) was packed, and Jackie Wilson was in the middle of his performance. One guy in the audience was beating on the woman he was with, perhaps enraged with her enthusiasm for the singer.

"After awhile, it got next to Jackie. He jumped off the stage, went through the crowd standing and staring in disbelief. I think he went upside the home boy's head once or twice and that was it. Jackie then leaped back on stage and continued his show.

"Jackie Wilson was a bad boy during that time. He was a Golden

Glove in his past, you know, I heard."

Singer Toni Lynn Washington recalled that she had done some openings for Jackie in the early 1960s. Her record company, Conti, hooked her up to perform some openers for him in the South—Mississippi, New Orleans, Alabama—to promote her single *Dear Diary.* "He was very exciting. A very open person. I didn't have too many personal contacts with him but he was a very nice person. He was like a superstar then. It would be the same as opening for Michael Jackson."

Ms. Washington remembered Jackie had a medical team that was traveling with him, a doctor and a nurse. "Once, when I opened for him in New Orleans, he was very sick. I think it was pneumonia. He did the show anyway, but he had to be carried off the stage. He was amazing. I used to get a big kick out of Jackie kissing all the girls after the show."

One of Jackie's most intriguing characteristics was that he appeared so different to everyone, even those who spent a lot of time with him and knew him well. George saw a totally different side of Jackie than Murry described, but even his description is contradictory as to the duality of Jackie's personality. "Well, to me he was one of the most fascinating entertainers I ever saw because the years I worked for Jackie and the months and the years, nights, and days we traveled together he was always the same. He was generous. I mean, he was nice. I mean, he would stop on the street and sign an autograph. He would shake your hand, but he would fight, too, if you made him mad."

Both Gorgeous George and Jackie's valet, Frazier, confirm Jackie suffered from both the pain of having a bullet lodged in his body, and the fear it might someday dislodge and cause a serious medical problem. It is easy to imagine that fear alone would cause Jackie to tame his flamboyant stage act. Jackie often complained of shoulder pain and Frazier felt it caused Jackie to rely on the deadening of sensation created by drugs, marijuana, and alcohol. Any proclivity Jackie showed toward these habits prior to the shooting intensified afterward.

To further complicate Jackie's life, he and Harlean were divorced after only two years of marriage. A news report in the March 22, 1969, issue of the **Amsterdam News** disclosed Jackie's constant travel schedule as a reason for the breakup, but other sources claim Jackie either caught or suspected Harlean and Tarnopol of having an affair. He filed for the divorce and it was agreed between them he would pay support and education for Petie. Whether this precipitated his disillusion with Tarnopol or not, it certainly contributed to his growing distrust of his manager and the disintegration of their relationship.

Harlean was residing with Petie in the couple's $600 per month, five-room penthouse apartment on Broadway after Jackie moved to a low-rent Manhattan apartment, but she intended to move to the suburbs once the divorce was final. Following the divorce, Jackie began drinking heavily and smoking marijuana. He would remain in his apartment for days without dressing or venturing outside. He continued to owe support and alimony to Freda even as his debts to

Harlean began to accrue. Ten years later, in an interview with Al Duckett for *Sepia* magazine, Harlean gave her version of the Jackie Wilson she knew. The stated purpose of the interview was an attempt to dispel the many negative comments being made about Jackie, in particular that he was a dope addict and most of the money he earned went into his arm. She denied accusations that Jackie was arrogant, claiming he was softhearted unless pressed. She felt he was friends with the people who worked for him and sometimes people took advantage of that. She also brushed aside rumors of his Gemini dual personalities.

Harlean also wanted to dispel complaints he was irresponsible, didn't pay his bills and was habitually late for shows. (After appearing seven times, Ed Sullivan is said to have ceased inviting Jackie to perform on his show because he was repeatedly late.) Mrs. Wilson surmised perhaps the people he hired to work for him were irresponsible. She denies that he made unreasonable demands on how he was to be presented by emcees and promoters.

When asked what kind of a person he was she replied: "Well, I would have to say he was genuinely concerned about other people. He had a soft spot, sometimes perhaps a little too soft. But Jackie truly was devoted to his fans and anxious to help others get ahead. He always recognized his good fortune and he certainly went out of his way to help others who were having more of a problem in getting into the industry than he did. . . He never forgot his roots. Never forgot who he was and how his fame came about and the people who first accepted him."

Bill Murry recalls exactly what roots Harlean referred to. "He told me to come to this little small nightclub [in Detroit] where he was working. And when I came there I didn't recognize him because he had on this silk shirt and tie and was down on his knees singing *Danny Boy*. He had on a dark suit with a big patch where Mama Wilson had patched the knee of it for him. And he'd get down on his knees so that people couldn't see that patch on one knee."

Jackie's third wife, Lynn, also spoke kindly of the private man. "I loved Leroy Wilson. Jackie Wilson was fine, but I loved Leroy. I loved the human being. We had a life outside of Jackie Wilson, and that is what I wanted him remembered for. Not to take anything away from him being a great artist, but he was a great humanitarian. We'd be walking down the street and if a child needed a pair of shoes, he'd give him money to go buy shoes."

After years of adoration by women and people telling him he was the greatest, Jackie had added a drop of arrogance to his attitude. Murry recalled, "I remember one time in Cleveland they had him and Gene Chandler as headliners and on the marquee. They had the names side by side, and he waited until five minutes before he got ready to go on to call me to say he wasn't going on, and I asked why. He said, 'Did you look at that marquee?' So we had to stop the show, pay the stagehand an extra $16, which was the hourly wage at the time, to go out there and change the marquee and put his name above Gene Chandler's. And then he went on."

Lamar Cochran was a combination valet/chauffeur for Jackie at the time he was shot. As part of Jackie's entourage, he performed the same duties as Frazier and J.J. His view of Jackie was tempered with obvious admiration: "As a rule he was a wonderful young fella. If he had a few dollars in his pocket we had to keep an eye on him because if someone had a sad story out it came. He was very aggressive in doing this. . . he had a very big heart. . . he was like what you call a big soft touch. . . he loved people. . . he had to get a kiss from all the females and babies and so forth. And he loved animals. He was crazy about dogs. . . . He was like Jackie Robinson. He made it possible for all the black players in the league. . . .

Cochran does not pull punches when it came to Jackie's vices. He related how they would carry a few pounds of marijuana in the trunk of the car which Frazier would roll into joints and keep in a cigarette box. He confirmed Jackie had a cocaine habit that got so out of hand at times they had to lock him in a room "until he decided to get himself together." Frazier stated that in order to keep up with Jackie you had to stay on some kind of speed. "Man, you would have to be doing something to keep up with him. You know what I'm talking 'bout? You'd have to be on black beauties, had to be somewhere out there to keep up."

Cochran also confirms Jackie's drug abuse escalated after the shooting. "Jackie had a [Cadillac] limousine. We had block out windows in it. He had a big bear rug in the back so he could stretch out or he could have him some little piece of ass back there and let the partition up in the front for privacy. He carried all his medicine and everything with him. We kept a case of CC (Canadian Club) in the trunk for him and soda and all his stomach medicine and what-ever. We used to go by the Henry Hudson Hotel in New York and pick up his prescription. . . like a magnesia thing that was snow white that the doctor would fix up, this was right after he got shot."

Despite the drugs and questionable personal ethics, there are many instances of Jackie coming to someone's aid in their time of need. Once such incident occurred when Jesse Belvin was killed. Belvin, best known for composing the Penguins hit *Earth Angel*, was traveling with Jackie on the road to a show in Dallas. The musicians were in a caravan with Jackie in front being driven by his valet, Frazier. Jesse was in the middle car with his wife, Jo Ann, being driven by Charles, his chauffeur. Charles fell asleep at the wheel and hit an oncoming car head on. Both Charles and Jesse were killed instantly, but Jo Ann was alive. Jackie was a few miles up the road and did not know the tragedy happened behind him.

Etta James states in her autobiography, "They rushed the bodies to a hospital. Knowing Charles and Jesse were dead, their main concern was for Jo Ann. But the hospital, run by white doctors, wanted to know who was paying. No one had enough money. Jo Ann was left unattended with a crushed pelvis, a crushed chest, a broken arm. She was left in a coma until they could reach Jackie Wilson in Dallas. Jackie drove back to Arkansas to pay the doc-tors."

Jo Ann never recovered and died of her injuries. Jackie sang at their funeral but, according to Etta,". . . he was so broke up he could barely make a sound."

"He was going to be bigger than Sam Cooke," Etta said of Belvin. "Bigger than Nat Cole. He was heading in that direction."

Bob Thiele felt, in hindsight, had Jackie been with Motown during this period, Gordy would have taken a more active role in Jackie's personal life and kept him from his spiral of self-inflicted abuse. "Well, we know he was involved with drugs. I don't say that he had the best guidance in all areas. I'm not talking about recording, because I'm not going to say we were making lousy records. We were making good records. But I would say in all other aspects of his career, I think he was misguided. I don't think he was treated properly from a financial aspect, I can't even talk about it. But knowing the business as I do, I'm sure he wasn't seeing all the dollars he made, even though he got some new clothes and a new car and things like that. But he was also getting drugs. So maybe Motown would have been better. . . I think it would have been better in a guidance sense. Because as I know the story, Berry Gordy and people like that, they really controlled the lives of those artists, which was a new approach at the time."

But stories of Jackie's big heart and loyalty are peppered throughout reminiscences of the people who know and often loved Jackie. In May 1960 he teamed up with Johnny Cash and Dizzy Gillespie to play at Boston University to raise funds for students expelled for demonstrating. Frazier estimated Jackie gave away at least $20,000 in jewelry. "Yeah, he was Mr. Excitement. I'm saying that he would wear diamond cuff links from Phil Kronfield and like a $200, $300 suit, and sometimes ties, $25 ties, and like he would just throw it out there [into the crowd]." Frazier recalled how women were constantly tearing at his shirts and trying to remove his diamond wrist watch.

Insiders also say Jackie bought most of his fancy custom stage attire from haberdasher Phil Kronfield, that he paid for all of it out of his own pocket, and that he was constantly giving them away. Gorgeous George, an admitted clothes horse, recalled, "I was into clothes. I didn't never want to see an act go on the stage with pants wrinkled. And I might have had 30 suits in my dressing room. Jackie used to come in my dressing room and if he liked something I had, he loved black shirts, and he'd see something I had and we want to go to a party, he'd come put on something of mine. And he might have a new suit in a bag and he said, 'George any suit that you see me tear, you can have the suits.' He used to give me so many suits. He had given me dozens. New or tore. Because I used to take the suit, stitch it and you never would notice. I would change the buttons and I used to wear sequin coats and glass coats, platinum coats."

Bill Murry confirmed George used to repair all the clothes Jackie had torn off him by his adoring fans. It wasn't just his shirts, either. One time when Jackie was walking around with shredded pants, Murry told him, "Man, your butt is hanging out. And he looked at me and said, that's the fashion.'"

Frazier recalled Jackie would sometimes give away $1,000 to $1,500 a day, but his generosity went deeper that merely giving away money and material possessions. Etta James, in her autobiography, recalls a time when she and Jackie were playing at the

Howard in Washington with James Brown as the headliner. Brown, who grew up in a brothel and spent time as a juvenile delinquent, was a control freak and orchestrated everyone's position, on and offstage. Brown asked Etta to go out and buy him some socks, and Etta was a few minutes late getting back to the Howard for their afternoon performance, so he fired her from the show. When she tried to explain, he said she had a big mouth and that she was fired.

"'If she goes, then I'm going too.' It was Jackie Wilson saving my ass again! 'Frazier,' he said to his valet, 'start packing.'

"James knew he couldn't carry the show by himself. He needed Jackie, and Jackie, that loyal dog, was ready to walk on my behalf.

"I spent lots of time with Jackie Wilson. Jackie was different. . . . He had a skittish personality— fiery and unpredictable. You didn't threaten or cross Jackie. And it wouldn't take much to get his fists to flying. He had a 'don't-fuck-with-me vibe' that most everyone respected. I loved being invited over to his house in Detroit or his apartment at the Sire Arms on 57th Street in midtown Manhattan. It was always the Jackie Wilson show—onstage and off—but I didn't mind. You'd get there and Frazier would let you in, sit you in the living room, offer you some wine or weed. Jackie's records would be playing—*Lonely Teardrops, Night, Doggin' Around, Baby Workout, Talk That Talk*—and then an hour or so later Jackie would stroll in, talking about Jackie—he'd just done this, he'd just done that. He was cordial and charming as could be—I know Jackie cared for me—but Jackie was incapable of talking about anything but Jackie. Jackie Wilson loved being Jackie Wilson."

Overall Etta had mostly positive words to say about Jackie because he was always coming to her rescue. '[In Missouri] I opened for Jackie to a packed house. The audience dug me. But when I went to get my money, the promoter shrugged his shoulders and said the gate was so disappointing he couldn't pay. I was fit to be tied. My plan was to take this money and buy me and Abye bus tickets for Chicago where, after all the talk from Bobby Lester of the Moonglows, I wanted to meet the Chess brothers and get me a new record deal. I wanted to wring this promoter's neck, but the more I shouted, the more he shrugged. He wouldn't give me a dime.

"By the time we got through arguing, Jackie had come offstage. When he saw what was happening with me, he reached in his pocket and paid me himself. On another occasion when Murray the K was about to kick me off the bill at the Brooklyn Paramount for talking back to him, Jackie stepped in, called his valet, Frazier, who came from the Midnighters, and said, 'Pack my bag. I'm leaving with Etta.' Murray the K shut up real quick. So God bless Jackie Wilson. He got me to Chicago."

In looking into the life of Jackie Wilson, media accounts of Jackie's heyday years generally confirm the present-day recollections of the people Jackie knew. They describe him as a "wonderful young fella," a "nice guy", a "soft-touch," and a "loyal friend." With the exception of isolated displays of arrogance and egotism, all the negative aspects of Jackie's persona seem purely self-destructive—unless you consider the totally different Jackie Wilson who appears in **Don't Block the Blessing—Revelations of a Life-**

time: The Autobiography of Patti LaBelle (Lady Marmalade, If Only You Knew).

"We [Patti LaBelle and the Bluebells] were appearing at a theater in Brooklyn on the bill with America's heartthrob, Jackie Wilson. . . Jackie could move like James Brown—the splits, the spins, the slides. And he could sing like Sam Cooke—that pure, clear amazing voice. With his back-flips, his knee-drops, and his golden voice, he would drive the women so wild they would literally rip the shirt off his back just trying to touch him. Like everyone else, I was in awe of him. I worshiped the stage he moved on.

"My adoration changed to hatred in a dark corner of Brooklyn's Brevoort Theater one terrifying night."

As Patti made her way down an unlit hallway toward the stage for her performance, someone grabbed her and said, "I've been wanting you for a long time." Patti recognized the voice as Jackie's.

"He started kissing my neck, and I could smell the liquor on his breath. As I struggled to free myself, Jackie's accomplice started dragging me backwards. I was kicking with all my might, but I was no match for him. Here I was, this little five-foot-three-inch girl up against this 250-pound sweaty, funky gorilla. Suddenly, he stopped dragging me. I heard a door shut. It was the sound of doom.

"I was their prisoner. No one knew I was in trouble . . . Jackie went first."

Patti claims her prodigious vocal ability saved her. When she screamed loudly, Jackie and his unidentified accomplice fled. Patti's virtue remained intact, but ". . . after the nightmare, I would see

Jackie on the circuit from time to time, I never spoke to him again. For years, before I learned the power of forgiveness, I hated that man. I couldn't bring myself to look at him. I never could understand why a man who was so loved would try to force himself on a young admirer."

Spotlight on…
Jackie Wilson

The following series of photos are an example of a typical live performance by "Mr. Excitement."

Jackie hits the stage stylishly dressed in coat and tie and the audience goes into an immediate frenzy.

After shedding his coat and tie (often thrown to the crowd), Jackie drops to his knees during a slow love song while pleading for love.

An emotional female fan rushes to the side of her heart throb.

Unable to control herself, she wants more from the
"World's Greatest Rock & Roll Performer"
as Jackie's body guards stand by.

As things get out of control, and more females
charge the stage to get a piece of the action,
the bodyguards go to work.

...and, as usual, when things reach a fevered pitch,
Jackie Wilson disappears from view.

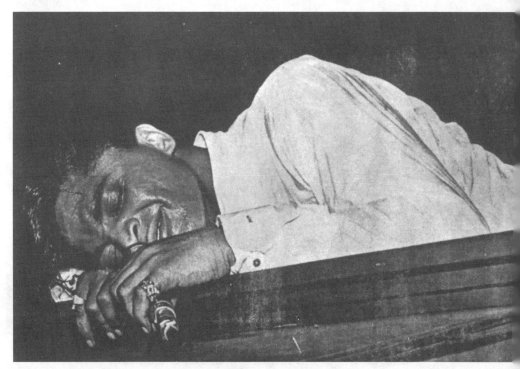

...but the show goes on!

Jackie, with manager Nat Tarnopol, and radio personality, Alan Freed. Freed, who coined the phrase, "Rock and Roll," is also credited with giving Jackie Wilson the name, "Mr. Excitement."

Jackie sings "You Better Know It" in the 1959 movie, "Go, Johnny, Go."

Leaving Roosevelt Hospital in New York city on March 18, 1961. Jackie was shot by Juanita Jones in the early morning hours following Valentines Day, February 15, 1961. That's his wife, Freda (rt.) and his mother, Eliza Lee.

Jackie with Alfred Hitchcock and Gregory Peck at Hugh Hefner's mansion in the early '60s.

From Billboard's *Winter Spotlight,* December 19, 1960.

Billboard Magazine June 8, 1959

"The Album Covers"

From 1957 to 1975, Brunswick Records released thirty-two Jackie Wilson albums.

These are the cover photos from the author's private collection.

See Release Dates on pages 248 and 249.

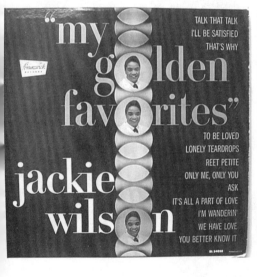

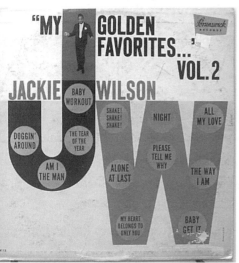

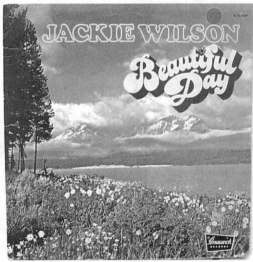

These are the only two photographs known to be circulated of Elvis Presley and Jackie Wilson together.

Elvis and Jackie on the movie set "Spinout." Elvis signed a photo like this one, "Jackie, you got a friend for life."

On August 18, 1974, Elvis took 19 of his friends to see Jackie's performance on Dick Clarks' "Good ol' Rock 'n Roll Review" in the casino lounge of the Las Vegas Hilton Hotel. This photo was taken in Elvis' private suite on the 30th floor of the Hilton Hotel.

GORGEOUS GEORGE

Jackie's favorite mcee, Gorgeous George, was interviewed for this book.

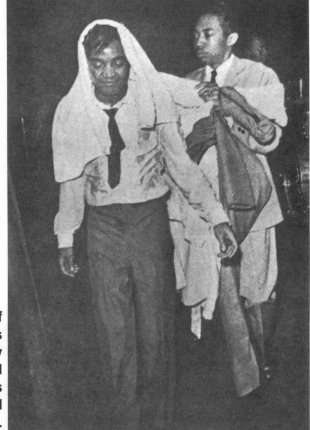

Jackie is led off stage in his heyday by personal valet Bill Frazier, who was also interviewed for this book.

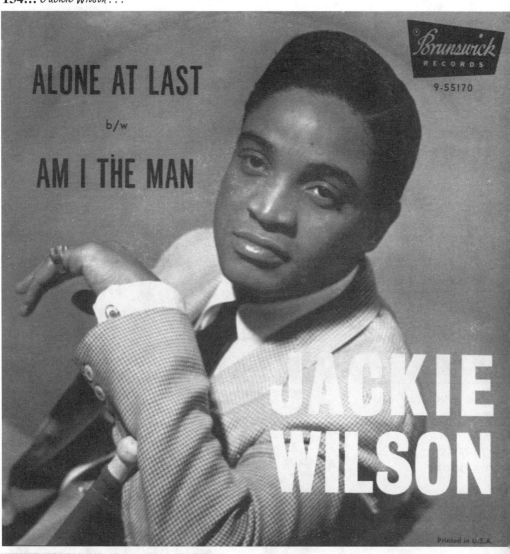

ALONE AT LAST

b/w

AM I THE MAN

JACKIE WILSON

Brunswick
RECORDS
9-55170

Printed in U.S.A.

BILLY WARD
and the
DOMINOES

A COLLECTION OF RARE ALBUM TRACKS AND SINGLE SIDES

Jackie Wilson

THROUGH THE YEARS

Hall of Fame Inductees LaVern Baker and Jackie Wilson had a minor hit in 1965 with "Think Twice." A wild, hard-to-find X-rated version exists.

Chapter Six

"Get Baby for Me"
(So Many) Cute Little Girls

Because Patti LaBelle did not come forth with her revelations until 1996, we will never know Jackie's side of what occurred behind the Brevoort Theater stage. Despite marriage vows, Jackie did not remain faithful to any of his wives. Despite being shot by a spurned lover, Jackie continued to make a career of tantalizing women, driving them to the edge of reason. He was incredibly handsome with a warm smile and bright, shining eyes. He wore tight, well-tailored suits, and wingtip shoes. He favored black shirts and ties and groomed himself with purpose in the manner most attractive to women of the sixties, who were just beginning to feel the first wave of sexual liberation. During his stage acts he sweated and swooned, exuding sexuality and engineering musical seduction into an art form.

Beverly Lee of the Shirelles remembers Jackie performing at the Apollo: "He would always bring the house down when he sang

To Be Loved, and they put the little red pinlight on him. He drove the women crazy. We were friends with him, and we were drooling. But he was always a very warm and friendly person. He's magnetic. He had such drawing power. He loved to greet you with a nice kiss and a smile; always up and up, a lot of energy. He was like a very slinky powerful leopard on-stage. There was nothing he couldn't do there. He was very sexy. When he would do his little shadowboxing as I call it—his little movements, and the way he handled the mike—he was just amazing." A cut from the LP, **Baby Workout**, *(So Many) Cute Little Girls* could have been Jackie's theme song.

Admiration of Jackie is by no means limited to women. In his autobiography, Berry Gordy, Jr., recalls the first time he saw Jackie perform—at a concert at the Armory in Flint, Michigan. "I had never seen anything like that in my life. Crowds pushing and shoving to get into the sold-out house. I had heard Jackie was known as Mr. Excitement. When he hit the stage, I could see why. It was like a lightning bolt. Strutting and dancing with his coat slung over his shoulder singing *Reet Petite*, spinning and turning, he jumped off one level of the stage to another, landing in a perfect split. I was worried like many others that he had to have hurt something. But without stopping he squeezed his legs together and propelling himself up into a standing position just in time to do another twirl, drop to his knees, and finish the song.

"Jackie had worked himself and the audience into a frenzy. He was sexy and knew it. I could tell by the way he winked his eye at the front-seated women right on beat. I had never seen women throw panties on stage before.

"He was Mr. Excitement! Even at the end of the show, his energy was still flowing like electricity, body pouring with sweat, his shirt hanging open—and me helping him off stage as women were trying to jump all over him."

Throughout the years Bill Murry saw Jackie at his very best and his most degenerate. He told how Jackie would consume an 8-ounce glass of scotch before going on stage, and it made him sweat profusely. "Jackie was an alcoholic, and Jackie was a very cocky, arrogant-type person. He was like a male Billie Holiday. If he liked you, he was the best friend you could have. If he didn't like you, you had one of the worst enemies you could have. His mannerisms were crude and if AIDS had been a problem back then, Jackie would have never made it to be thirty years old because Jackie had an obsession for women. During Jackie's performance, he'd have to French kiss somebody on the floor or he wasn't satisfied. Women knew this, and they used to just run to him by the dozen and just tear his clothes off, kissing and laying it on. He had to always be with some woman. That night he got shot, he was with a woman he didn't want to be bothered with the next day. He degraded the woman, and she shot him. But he had to be with somebody every night." In his lust for the attention of women, Jackie was very much like Elvis.

Murry also recalled how Jackie's promiscuity resulted in a nationwide brood of illegitimate children. When asked how many kids he had altogether, Murry replied, "We haven't got that much time." But he did recall a night he met one of Jackie's children." Jackie was going down real bad and the last kid he has was with a white girl. I was in Cleveland working in a nightclub called Neil's Casino . . . and he came in with this girl and had this baby. The baby was fourteen-days-old.

"The next night when I went to work I went to the drugstore to get a toy for the baby, and I wound up getting a big old plastic hammer, a mallet. And the baby was throwing it around with one hand I said, 'Damn, he looks like the mighty Thor, you know.' And Jackie said, 'That's what I'm going to name him.' And he did." Murry found this absurd and decided it was time to take his leave. "So I had it, I never saw Jackie again after that."

Gorgeous George readily confirmed Jackie's addiction to women. "Well, there would be about 400 women lined up, and he would kiss all 400 of them. If there was a thousand, he would kiss a thousand. Night after night."

At least part of Jackie's behavior toward women was prompted by the profit motive. Frazier offered the following insight: "He kissed the ugliest girl in the crowd. I think his saying was, like, mostly the ugliest girls will buy the records. You know what I'm talking about? And so he would kiss the ugliest girl in the audience and the girls would be sitting 'round the dressing room like mad."

Billy Vera, on the album cover for *Jackie Wilson Through the Years*, confirmed Frazier's assertion that there was a bit more to Jackie's love of women than merely the promise of sex. "Jackie as always, was brilliant. He sang his ass off, danced like both Nicholas Brothers, and made every woman in the house think he was singing only to her, raising the excitement level of the female half of the audience to such heights that any man who didn't get lucky with his date or wife that night didn't try.

"Many a time I saw Jackie on his back, lean his head over the edge of the Apollo Theater stage offering to kiss the least attractive woman in the place.

"'Billy, if I kiss the ugliest one in the house, they'll all think they can have me and keep comin' back and payin'—just to get their greasy lips wrapped around my face.'

"What a showman. Jackie's bathroom sink had more bottles of mouthwash and antiseptic than I've ever seen anywhere else. Understandably, he developed a phobia of germs. Still, he felt, whatever is the best for the show. . . .

"Jackie was the coolest, sharpest cat on Broadway. He had a smile for all, and if he didn't remember your name, you got a new one: 'Baby.'"

Showmanship or lust? Sometimes, as Frazier recalled, Jackie would "take up" with a girl from time to time, and apparently, more than one at a time. "He didn't care what all of them would think; they would all be there and see if they could be with him tonight 'cause at that time, like, well say within New York, maybe you'd start in the morning at the first show and you didn't come out until that night. Talking about two, three shows a day. And then, as hard as Jackie worked at that time, on a weekend he might do six shows.

It wouldn't be that long, but you'd be there until at least 'bout 12, 1 that night 'fore you'd get out and then Jackie would drink B&B, you know, or we might be up. I've seen him stay up a whole week, you know, all day, all night.

"Oh, if they be pretty girls he might take them somewhere to a girl's house and you'd stay in the car till he gets ready and he comes back out and we'd probably go back home or something like that to his apartment, 'cause at that time he had an apartment on 57th Street. And we would go back there for a while and just try to lay down and get some shut eye or something. You know what I'm talking 'bout? 'Cause in the morning he had to be back up there again.

"His wife she never did come to New York. Freda didn't. She might come there to visit sometime. . . . Harlean was really his main choice."

It boiled down to all Jackie's associates attesting to his proclivity as a stud, including without hesitation, Lamar Cochran. "He was a guy that couldn't hold a conversation because it couldn't last that long, like he was a little shy other than being on stage. But he'd see a young lady or whatever and he just had to have her, he wants to make love to her or whatever. . . .

"Listen, if there is somebody at the show he wants to meet or when he'd go on stage and he'd see um, he would say 'Get baby for me.' Or somebody would come back and want an autograph, he'd be soaking wet, they won't hardly give you a chance to dry him off or let him change his clothes, but hell, he put his robe on.

They done ripped his shirt off on stage. And then he wants a cigarette and lay down and rest and somebody knock on the door. . . and he'd hear the voice. . .

"'I'm so and so, they told me up front that I could come back and get Jackie's autograph' and so forth. Jackie would say, 'Who is it? . . . Well, let baby in.' And she's got her friends with her and out of the three or four that would come in he got to kiss 'em all, got to stick his tongue down their throat. . . . They want to sit down now, and other people are trying to get in to see him. And his thing is, 'Baby's all right. Take her back out to the table and she's gonna meet us at such and such a place.' And she'd either be at the hotel or she'd ride in the car. . . . When they came to the hotel I would take all his jewelry from him and give him about $20 and he had all his calls transferred to my room.

"He had a couple [of women] he made a point to carry around somewhere, but normally each city had their own females for him. Sometimes he'd fly 'em across the country because they wanted to be with him.

"The only time I carried Jackie to California was when we drove there. He was on vacation to go chase pussy. Yeah. He was going with some girl out there named Madeline Allen. Very attractive young lady. She had the best body I ever saw on a female. She hooked me up with one of her girlfriends. We drove out to California in a chocolate Fleetwood. Boy, that was pretty. We stayed out there a couple of weeks and drove back to New York and Nat Tarnopol and Johnny Roberts would get him organized. At that time he did a lot of work for promoter Henry Winn. We'd do any-where from nineteen to twenty-five one-nighters."

It seemed all the men who knew Jackie envied his ability with women. Even Berry Gordy, Jr. Writing in his autobiography, Gordy dreamed, "If only I could be Jackie, just for a night."

"I thought about that more than once. Then, another night the strangest thing happened to me when one of the many girls who always seemed to be waiting for him asked me, 'Berry, why can't Jackie be more like you?'

"'What?!? What do you mean like me?'

"'You're so patient, understanding and easy to talk to. Jackie's not.'

"'Oh really. You think so? Maybe you'd like to go out with me?'

"Of course she said 'no.'

"Another time I was at a show of Jackie's and found myself seated next to the sweetest girl I'd seen in a long time. She had no eyes for me, but I kept doing everything I could to get her atten-tion. After a while, she softened, just enough to tell me she was not 'that kind of girl.'

"The more I persisted, the more she resisted. 'At least give me your phone number.'

"'I don't give my number out to nobody unless I know them really well.'

"We were having so much fun together watching the show be-fore Jackie came on. I tried to kiss her.

"'Oh, no,' she said, 'it wouldn't be proper.'

"'Not even on the cheek?'

"'Not even on the cheek.'

"I was impressed. She wasn't just a good girl, she was the perfect girl. Marriage was not out of the question.

"Needing to see Jackie before he went on stage I had to leave quickly. She agreed to meet me at the same spot right after the show.

"I returned breathlessly once the show was over and—nothing. Couldn't find her anywhere. Giving up, I headed back to the dressing room where, as usual, I saw a crowd of women around Jackie. And, as usual, there was one in the middle, clutching him for dear life, her tongue down his throat, her skirt pulled up around her waist. There she was in all her glory, my ex-future wife."

The phrase "sex, drugs and rock 'n roll" is not an accident. In books such as **Rock 'n Roll Confidential** and **Rock 'n Roll Babylon**, much has been written about the vacuous, amoral lifestyle led by the many rock stars that have risen since Jackie Wilson and Sam Cooke crooned their way in the hearts of millions of female fans. "Sex sells" is a widely accepted marketing credo and stars like Jackie Wilson and Elvis Presley were merely survivalist guinea pigs in a massive cultural experiment on gender exploitation.

Chapter Seven

The White Jackie Wilson

History did not record how Jackie Wilson came to be called "The Black Elvis," but both he and the White Elvis accepted the truth behind the title early in their careers. While Presley openly and enthusiastically praised Jackie's style and talent and admitted he was greatly influenced by Jackie's energy, Jackie also claimed, in a sort of modest mutual admiration society way, "I'd have to say that I got as much from him as he got from me."

All of Jackie's close associates confirm their stylistic ties as well. Bill Murry claimed, "A lot of people don't know it, but actually if you look at Elvis Presley real close, Elvis Presley used to try to be like Jackie Wilson."

G.C. Cameron, former lead singer of the Spinners, recalls, "Elvis was a friend of mine. Elvis lived around the corner from me when I lived in Beverly Hills. He loved Jackie; that's where he got a lot of his stuff from. People don't realize that. Jackie and Elvis were tight as a hatband."

Odell "Gorgeous" George recalled that Jackie and Elvis were

good friends and that "Elvis used to come and watch Jackie when we played Memphis and other places, Las Vegas, different places . . . He would come to the auditorium where we used to play. He used to stand right there at the end of the curtain and watch the show."

George also knew of the first time they met. Jackie approached Elvis and said, "They call me the black Elvis." And Elvis, who responded like a fan instead of the star he was in his own right, replied, "I thought it was about time the white Elvis Presley met the black Elvis Presley." Elvis would on occasion refer to himself as the "white Jackie Wilson."

Elvis and Jackie became close friends despite their racial differences, although those differences were really only skin deep. Elvis grew up surrounded by black children. He was fascinated by blues and gospel quartets and loved the rhythm and blues tunes sung by his neighbors. Besides the black influence on his singing, he also acquired a certain stance and a relaxed, loose-limbed walk uncommon to white men. A possible reason for their close friendship was revealed by Gorgeous George: "Elvis, man, was one of the nicest cats I ever met. He was just like one of us really. Matter of fact, he acted black to me. He was . . . he was a Southerner and he was just, you know, he was real."

In addition to a natural singing voice, Elvis's greatest talent was his ability to synthesize the sounds, looks, and musical abilities of others and unconsciously, or subconsciously as the case may be, make them a part of his own. He was aware of this aptitude and was always eager to attend performances of new talent, as well as passionate, established professionals like Sammy Davis, Jr. and Bobby Darin. The admiration of the full range of musical types was something Elvis shared with Jackie. In his interview with Norman Knight, Jackie claimed, "I like all types. Because, actually, well, if I'm available as you say, I'm off work. And I'm somewhere like Vegas or I might be in Lake Tahoe, well, I'd catch about anybody. But I just love Sammy Davis, I just love to watch him. When Sinatra was around, I'd always get me a front row seat. I didn't care where I was. If I was working—if I had one night off I'd go there. In fact, he did me a great favor once. I was playing Las Vegas, and I was at the Riviera, in the lounge, and he was at the Sands. We went down to see him once on an off night. After he finished the show . . . I'll never forget he had two big bands, Count Basie on one side of the stage and . . . Nelson Riddle on the other. There he was in the middle. He'd go over and do a number with Count and then with Nelson. After the show was over he walked off with the applause. Then he came back out, then he said, 'Sit down.'

'What's the matter?'

'I got something to tell you. There's a young man sitting in the front his name is Jackie—Jackie Wilson—you go see him. I'm coming down. You'll dig him.' It was great. Just like that. No more said. No more done. We walked off and you couldn't get in. They actually came down—everybody!"

Elvis often voiced his disdain for mechanical performers but praised any artist who felt the music first and then sang it, especially those, like Jackie, who put their all into their shows. He drew influence from everyone he encountered—from the truck drivers he worked with after high school to Hollywood actors—but never deliberately stole their stylistic techniques or imitated them.

Many of the major influences in his life were from blacks like Roy Hamilton and Bo Diddley. In **Elvis Aaron Presley: Revelations from the Memphis Mafia**, the foreman of the Memphis Mafia, Marty Lacker, said ". .. most of the singers Elvis really loved were black—Roy Brown, Jackie Wilson, Brook Benton, Billy Eckstine, Arthur Prysock, the Ink Spots, Roy Hamilton. And he absolutely loved black gospel."

In the same book, Billy Smith, Elvis's first cousin and companion until his death, is quoted as saying, "Elvis liked black artists. He liked the way Jackie Wilson sang and the way he moved.

"He kept up with how he was doing, even after Jackie had a stroke, I believe, in '75 and went into a coma. Now, he didn't like James Brown. He didn't like his attitude, and he didn't like his singing.

"He thought he was a screamer. He liked Jackie Wilson, and Clyde McPhatter, and Billy Ward and his Dominoes—all those guys."

Ironically, a rumor went around that Elvis was racist. According to Peter Guralnick, author of **Last Train to Memphis**, the highly acclaimed Presley biography, "The rumor that Elvis was a racist arose in the wake of his great success in 1956 and 1957. The story was investigated by Jet [the black weekly] and found to be untrue. Elvis articulated again and again his admiration for black music and black artists." In the August 1, 1957, issue of **Jet** magazine, reporter Louie Robinson wrote that Elvis thinks "people are people, regardless of race, color or creed."

A story illustrates the depth of his feeling. He was performing with the black group Sweet Inspirations in Mississippi when the audience started throwing pennies on the stage. Elvis felt this was a sign of blatant racism and wanted to cancel the rest of the shows, until the Sweet Inspirations convinced him it was not that they were black, it was that the audience was displeased because they could not see Elvis whenever they stepped forward.

Elvis spent part of his youth in Memphis where shows were still segregated between blacks and whites. Elvis often attended the black shows and began to blend their cool African-American ways with the growing white teen idol craze and the rebels-with-a-cause like James Dean and Marlon Brando. All these performers had one thing in common—visceral sexuality—and Elvis solidified all of them into one handsome, explosive package that just happened to be able to sing and act.

Elvis Aaron Presley was born in Tupelo, Mississippi, on January 8, 1935, seven months after Jackie Wilson was born in Detroit. He attended First Assembly of God Church with his parents and sang gospel, just like Jackie. His fifth grade teacher discovered his singing ability and informed the school's principal, who entered Elvis in the talent contest at the Mississippi-Alabama Fair and Dairy

Show on October 3, 1945, where Elvis won second place singing *Old Shep.*

Although Elvis loved to sing at an early age, he did not pursue his talent vigorously until August 1953 when he dropped in at the Memphis recording studio during his lunch break. The studio manager, Marion Keisker, allowed him to record two songs—*My Happiness* and *That's When Your Heartache Begins.* Before he was halfway through the first song, Keisker knew Elvis had the sound the studio was looking for—"A white singer with a Negro voice." The studio owner, Sam Phillips, felt Elvis had some talent but needed work. Over a year later, on July 7, 1954, Phillips took a recording of *That's All Right (Mama)* to local radio station WHBQ. The response was so overwhelming the disk jockey tracked Elvis down until he found him at a movie theater and brought him back to the radio station for an on-the-air interview.

Elvis was an immediate sensation in Memphis but received lukewarm responses in several live performances after that. He had signed a contract with Phillips, but in a prime example of a poor business decision, Phillips sold it to RCA, although Phillips defends the decision to this day. Colonel Tom Parker, a former carnival worker who had been instrumental in the RCA contract negotiations, took over management of Elvis in late 1954. His first recording session with RCA produced, among others, his first big hit—*Heartbreak Hotel.*

According to the authors of **Elvis: What Happened?**, " . . . with the exception of the music of Bill Haley, urbanized rock &

roll radio remained virtually all black until the coming of Elvis Presley early in 1956." Jackie's associate, Bill Murry, reveals what happened behind the scenes as the dividing line between black and white music began to blur. "Colonel Parker kept all the attention on Elvis down because everybody thought [he was] a black artist and all the black people were running out and buying *Heartbreak Hotel*. But they didn't know he was white and then when the record starting going good, Colonel Parker released pictures that he was white and white people came out of the closets and started buying black music. Back before Elvis Presley, white people used to buy what they called brown bag music, and **Billboard** never carried any advertisements on blacks except maybe one little paragraph that would say, "Race Music," maybe Jackie Wilson's *Lonely Teardrops* or Louis Jordan's *Don't Worry About the Music*. That was it. And white people played it, but played it in low tones where the neighbors wouldn't hear it. And after Elvis Presley they pumped the volume up. And everybody came back. Fats Domino came back, Little Richard came back."

Within three months of *Heartbreak Hotel* Elvis was auditioning in Hollywood and had appeared on television on the *Milton Berle Show* and the *Steve Allen Show*. But it was his appearance on the *Ed Sullivan Show* in front of fifty-four million viewers, over one-third of the entire population of the United States, that launched his meteoric career.

Immediately after his first television appearance on the *Milton Berle Show* there was a vociferous backlash of public sentiment over his burlesque hip gyrations and phallic guitar, or what **Time** writer Richard Corliss in his article "From Hound Dog to Lounge Act" so aptly called "the pulverizing novelty of sexual danger." White adults declared Elvis' blatant sexuality too provocative for the legions of teenage girls who, in their parents' eyes at least, seemed to turn overnight from bobby-socked coeds and demure debutantes into screaming, swooning hoards of libidinous harlots. Unlike blacks, who embraced the sensuality of music, this was far too much for WASPS still clinging to the genealogy and mores of their Puritan ancestors. Elvis was quickly and permanently domesticated into the mainstream. According to Corliss, " . . . his movie and music producers, and the Colonel, called the shots in what should have been Elvis's prime. He didn't rebel; he did it their way."

Elvis proved to be very adept at going along with whatever the script called for. For a Hollywood screen test he "finger-synced" through *Blue Suede Shoes* on a guitar with no strings. When they asked him to clean up his act, dress up in a tuxedo, and croon *You Ain't Nothing But a Hound Dog* to a basset hound on the **Steve Allen Show** in 1956, he did it with confidence. Elvis was already so professional in his demeanor, watching tapes of that show you cannot tell that to him, as he would later claim, "It was the most ridiculous performance of my career." His acting was so natural it came across as truly high class.

All this obedience and acquiescence from the very symbol of masculinity and rebellion took a toll on the sense of pride and strength that made Elvis so admired by young people searching for a role model. Sadly, within a few short years, Elvis was reduced to doing Elvis, playing himself in his nightclub acts and movies—the first true Elvis impersonator.

Elvis made twenty-seven movies during the 1960s decade. But according to Fred L. Worth and Steve D. Tamerius in their book **Elvis: His Life from A to Z**, " . . . musically, the mid-1960s was a period of decline for Elvis. None of his singles released reached number one and almost all of them were from his movies. His records weren't the giant hits they were in his golden years of the 1950s and early 1960s. Elvis's decline can be attributed to several factors. Foremost among them is the advent of the British invasion and, specifically, the Beatles. The sheer number of instrumental and vocal groups and single performers on the music charts simply diluted the market. There was more competition for the public's record-buying dollar, and it took a much stronger record to reach number one or to become a million seller."

Like Elvis, Jackie's record sales and his career were also affected when millions of record-buying youths began looking across the sea at the totally new sound of the English rockers and, in addition to the factors already mentioned, this may have contributed to his personal and professional slump during those years. There is also the matter of time and priority. Elvis's management had him booked making movies, while Jackie's management had him on the road almost exclusively. From a strict marketing/publicity standpoint, the national exposure of movies versus the limited exposure of lounge acts and personal appearances should have certainly been a consideration. It is also a well-known fact in the entertainment world that road trips and constant touring is a tiring and debilitating existence. Jackie, one of the hardest working showman ever, was on a non-stop road trip. Sadly, one of the things he really wanted to try, but couldn't, was making movies.

Elvis first saw Jackie in 1956 when he was performing unbilled with Billy Ward and the Dominoes in Las Vegas. Later that year, at a Sun Records jam session, without the infamous Colonel around, Elvis spoke proudly of what he'd seen: "There's a guy out there who's doin' a take off on my *Don't Be Cruel*. He tried so hard till he got much better than that record of mine . . . He was a colored guy. . . . He grabbed that microphone, went down on the floor looking straight at the ceiling. Man, he cut me—I was under the table when he got through singing. Wooh! Man, he sang that song. I went back four nights straight and heard that guy do that. Man, he sang the hell out of that song."

In Joe Esposito and Elena Oumano's book, **Good Rockin' Tonight**, we learn about Elvis and Jackie's experience together in Hollywood. When in Hollywood Elvis "welcomed visitors but he almost never went out in public. One night, however, he made an exception. We went to The Trip, a club on La Cienega Boulevard next to the old Hollywood Playboy Club, because Elvis wanted to see Jackie Wilson, a big star at the time, known as 'Mr. Excitement' for his amazing voice and even more astounding performing ability. Elvis admired Wilson tremendously and had been deeply influenced by his style. The Trip barely held two hundred people, but James Brown was also in the audience that night, as were the Rolling Stones.

"When Jackie came off stage, the owner of the club and a friend of Elvis brought them four bottles of champagne. Elvis didn't usually drink the bubbly stuff, but he was having a good time and wanted to toast Jackie. Elvis and Wilson got along terrifically from their first meeting, and after Wilson's show, Elvis invited him to the studio for a few days while he was shooting the movie, *Double Trouble*. They talked a lot during Elvis's breaks, particularly about Wilson's ambition to act in films. The problem was that Jackie Wilson's management company, which was rumored to be associated with the Mafia, had its singer booked solid all year, mostly in its own clubs. Wilson never had three months free to do a film. Elvis identified with his dilemma. Like Elvis, Jackie was good-looking and intelligent, and the talent he longed to express was being wasted."

This incident is noteworthy for the fact that it was quite uncharacteristic for Elvis to invite anyone to his movie sets, but Elvis was as impressed with Jackie's persona and performance as with his music, and encouraged Jackie to consider acting. In fact, Elvis's real dream and goal in life was acting—serious acting, not the kind of fluff he ended up doing in most of his movies. Elvis showed tremendous dramatic potential from his very first screen test. Film directors who worked with Elvis report he always showed up on the set prepared, focused, and was dedicated to his acting career.

When movie producers realized the box office demand for his films, they began writing screenplays that incorporated his music.

Elvis was more in his element behind a camera than he ever was singing. He saw some of this latent talent in Jackie and encouraged him. There is little doubt Elvis could have arranged a screen test for Jackie but that would never be. Jackie told Elvis he would like to, but he was so booked up he didn't see how he would have time due to his long-term, airtight contract, making him essentially the exclusive property of Brunswick Records.

Jackie and Elvis became fast friends forever and the cosmic conjunction of their names became a part of their shared legend. There was such a revolving door between the two stars that Jackie, during his tenure with Billy Ward and the Dominoes, felt free to add Elvis's songs to their stage act. In a preserved tape of a rare Presley/Carl Perkins/Jerry Lee Lewis/Johnny Cash jam session called The Million Dollar Quartet made at Sun Records on December 4, 1956, Presley remarks that he watched Jackie's act six times and again raved about Jackie's performance of Elvis's hit song, *Don't Be Cruel.* Elvis said on the tape he wished he had recorded it in that style, then turned right around and adopted Jackie's enhancements as his own. On January 4, 1957, Elvis appeared on the **Ed Sullivan Show** for the third and final time. He sang a medley of his biggest hits ending with a rendition of *Don't Be Cruel* which imitated Jackie's interpretation, including finger rolls and a jazzed up finale.

The black and the white Elvis had many encounters over the years; some of the time it involved them helping each other out in some way. More often it was Elvis coming to watch Jackie perform. In **Elvis: What Happened**?, co-author Sonny West recalled, "Jackie Wilson, the singer, was a good friend of ours. He was a very nice dude, and the people who worked for him were very close to us. Anyway one of the guys who knew him (Johnny Roberts) called me up and told me there was something he wanted to talk to me about. Well, I went over to the Flamingo Hotel, where Jackie was playing, and this guy who knew Jackie introduces me to two guys. They were from New York, if you know what I mean. This was at the end of 1973, and Elvis used to get a lot of massages from a guy who worked for one of the hotels. I won't say which because that would identify him. But this guy used to get a hundred dollar tip from Elvis every time he massaged him. Also, Elvis would sign a chit and it was in triplicate. This guy not only got paid and tipped, he had a scheme where he would present the bill twice, until I caught up with him. So, he was a con man right from the word go. I'll just call this guy 'Big Bill' (which is not his real name).

"Anyway, it seems one of these guys from New York was getting a massage, and this Big Bill starts shooting his mouth off to him that he has massaged Elvis Presley and that he [Elvis] is a head [drug-taker]. My mind gets buzzing and I think, if Big Bill told a perfect stranger this, how many people has he told? Well, the guy, who knew Jackie Wilson, says that he is telling me this because he knows how much Jackie Wilson loves Elvis, and I thank him for his concern."

Elvis followed Jackie's career for many years and was still showing up from time to time to watch him perform as late as 1974. Elvis's daily calendar for Sunday, August 18,1974, shows the following entry: "Elvis and nineteen of his friends attended a performance of Dick Clark's "Good Ol' Rock '*n* Roll Review" in the casino of the Hilton Hotel. Later, he met with Jackie Wilson, one of the stars of the Review."

Elvis never forgot his admiration for and perhaps the debt he owed Jackie indirectly. As Etta James tells it in **Rage to Survive**, "In a big club outside of Memphis, I shared a bill with Elvis Presley. I didn't know what to expect. He turned out supercool and extrarespectful with his 'pleased to meet you, ma'am' gentlemanly good manners. He also touched my heart many years later when my good friend Jackie Wilson was down and out, vegetating in some funky convalescent home. Elvis moved Jackie to a decent hospital and paid for everything."

It is well-known that when Jackie was in dire financial straits when Brunswick abandoned him after his stroke, Elvis sent Jackie's wife a check for $30,000 to help with his medical care. Like two planets orbiting the same star, the paths of Jackie and Elvis would cross many times. Although Jackie would never reach the heights of stardom his white counterpart achieved, the detrimental influences of their individual levels of fame and sacrifice would affect them in much the same way. As we will see, the reasons for this are many and varied but the results were tragically similar.

Chapter Eight

Passin' Through

While Elvis was in Los Angeles recording fourteen songs for the movie **Blue Hawaii** in March, 1961, Jackie was released from Roosevelt Hospital, and his records continued to grace the pop and R&B charts. While *Doggin' Around* hit the top of the R&B charts and #15 pop prior to his being shot, a song from the same recording session, *Please Tell Me Why*, did not reach US #20 until April 1961. The B-side *Your One and Only Love* made US #40. *Doggin' Around*, one of Jackie's few totally blues songs, was backed with *Night*, a totally operatic pop song backed by a horde of strings.

In July, *I'm Coming Back to You* reached US # 19 with the B-side *Lonely Life* making US #80. In September, *Years From Now* made US #37, while the B-side song, co-written by Wilson, *You Don't Know What It Means* peaked at US #79. Toward the fall of 1961, *The Way I Am* reached US #58, as the B-side *My Heart Belongs to Only You* peaked at US # 65.

Jackie also appeared in a black and white movie called **Teenage**

Millionaire, which featured musical performances by Dion, Marv Johnson, Chubby Checker, Vicki Spencer, and the Bill Black Combo. None of these performers had speaking roles. In fact, their performances were inserted throughout the movie without mention and done in what was described in the credits as "Musicolor," which appeared to be nothing more than a pale tint covering the screen. Jackie sang two songs: *The Way I Am* and *Lonely Life*. The cast included singer Jimmy Clanton, Rocky Graziano, Zasu Pitts, and Jack Larson. Clanton made a hit record without revealing his identity and Rocky played his body guard. Elvis saw the movie several times just to see Jackie's performance.

Jackie made some stylistic changes during the sixties by moving increasingly toward soul, while sprinkling a few operatic derivations of popular arias into his records. At the same time, he cultivated a high-gloss patina to spruce up his nightclub acts. This strategy was utilized by other rhythm and blues and rock 'n roll performers, trying to prolong their popularity, but it proved to be a dubious tactic.

One particular club date illustrates how far afield Jackie had strayed from his soul/rhythm and blues/rock 'n roll roots. The story was best told by Dick Jacobs in *Musician* magazine: "Jackie always had the ambition to transcend being a rock 'n roll singer and, as he put it, 'go on to bigger and better things.' So Nat Tarnopol booked Jackie for an engagement at the Fountainbleu Hotel in Miami Beach, opening for the deadpan comedian, Georgie Jessel.

"The crowd at the Fountainbleu was mainly your basic Borscht

Belt blue-hair-rinse set, who didn't know Jackie Wilson from James Brown. However, there was a sprinkling of hard-core Jackie fans at the shows. Jackie knew that the crowd was there mainly for Jessel, so he included an amazing punch-line to his set: a knockdown drag-out version of *My Yiddishe Momme*. And when this predominantly Jewish crowd got an eyeful of this black sylph gliding across the stage—like there's no such thing as gravity, and there's no bones in his body at all—and he's crooning a mean, mournful and exuberant *My Yiddishe Momme* that would stop a bar mitzvah cold before sending everybody's heart right through the ceiling, this polite but skeptical crew of Jessel fans went berserk. As a kind of insurance policy, we threw a couple of the standards like *California Here I Come* into the act and restricted the rock n' roll numbers to a long medley (to satisfy the real fans in the audience)."

According to Pruter: "Contemporary accounts of Wilson's high-toned supper club career were generally condescending, as one might expect from staid **Variety** critics. Said the reviewer of the Fountainbleu gig, 'This is rock *'n* roller Jackie Wilson's first turn in a demanding class nightery situation and he comes off in surprisingly good fashion . . . albeit in his first two offerings it seems he was going to turn out strictly rock *'n* roll . The shift to legit in terms of cafe song styling comes none too soon. Such balladings of *Night* and *Danny Boy* are well handled, but in a striving for too many tricky high-range effects tend to jar what are otherwise sock-reaction [sic] renderings.'"

Tarnopol also booked Jackie to headline at the Copacabana for one week in 1962. The Copa was the hottest nightclub in New York (perhaps in the world), and a live record was planned. The club was packed every night, and the show was a big success, but still Jackie could not wow the irascible **Variety** critic who wrote: "A handsome sepia youth with the frantic projection that is admired by teens, Wilson is none-the-less a shouter without the genuine musical gifts of many of his contemporaries."

It is hard to understand how Jackie could have viewed crooning *My Yiddishe Momme* and *California, Here I Come* as a bigger and better thing. Perhaps he was simply under the thrall of Nat's influence and echoing his manager's vision of the future of music, although Jacobs intimates it was all Jackie's idea. Perhaps Jackie just loved performing live no matter who was in the audience. There may be some truth here if you consider Jackie's comment to Norman Knight ". . . I did the same act. I never changed. The only difference was I'd wear the tuxedos in the major clubs, and at the rock and roll shows I'd wear the regular suits."

Or, it may have meant more to Jackie than just a change of clothing. Jackie is quoted on this subject on the album cover written by Ed Sullivan for *Jackie Wilson at the Copa*: "This Copa date came about sooner than Wilson and Tarnopol expected because Copacabana operator Jules Podell long-distanced them and asked if they could move up their date and rush into New York City to fill the vacancy created by the illness of Joey Bishop. In that engagement Wilson tore down the house and after the first show, Podell signed him immediately for dates three years ahead.

"'Ed, that was the thrill of a lifetime,' Jackie told me, after the opening show. 'When I walked out on that floor, so help me, I was a little bit scared. This was the floor on which Frank Sinatra, Martin & Lewis, Jimmy Durante, Sammy Davis, Jr., Joe E. Lewis, Rosemary Clooney, Lena Horne, Tony Martin, and all of those giants of our business had performed.

"'I think I must have felt the way a young ball player feels when he shows up in Yankee Stadium for the first time or steps into the Madison Square Garden ring for the first time or meets head-on Arnold Palmer in a golf tournament. It took me a couple of songs to get untensed, but from then on, I felt so happy and excited that I just sang up a storm.' But I guarantee that all of you who listen to this album, which Jackie Wilson recorded at the Copacabana, won't detect any trace of 'butterflies' in any of his vocal passages. The great ones of our business are always tense, facing each new challenge, but because they're great, they never exhibit it. This album was made right in the Copa with a regular Copacabana audience jamming the room. Wilson's all-time idol, Al Jolson, would have told Jackie that this was a top-flight job."

At any rate, Jackie was probably an active participant in Brunswick's crossover marketing scheme. In an interview conducted by Arnold Shaw in Jackie's dressing room at the Flamingo Hotel in Las Vegas, Jackie said, "Yeah, it's true I've recorded some things you don't expect from an R&B singer. But I don't know that I am an R&B singer. Sure, black people buy my records—just look at the R&B charts—but so do white people. I've had Gold Records, and I played the Copa in the early sixties before they were saying black is beautiful.' Some people say I'm a soul singer—and there is a lotta gospel in me.

"I'm proud that I have been accepted by the white world, but without losing my black audience. That's what counts—not losing your black fans. I'm not going to name names, but many black singers move away from their roots once they get the loot. I'm not a church goer, but I've got the gospel in me. Never do a show without 'Amen' as a closer. . . ."

During this period Jackie also found himself booked at the all-black Idlewild resort outside of Baldwin, Michigan. Idlewild was considered to be an all-black Catskills of sorts. Although it remained unmentioned in his autobiography, Berry Gordy spent summers there and many writers have claimed the kind of "middle of the road pastiche" he heard there eventually found its way into the cornucopia of sounds known as Motown.

According to emcee Bill Murry, "People came from as far as New York, Indiana, Jersey, Illinois, Michigan, and a few from other places. It was in the wilderness. This resort also had 18 days of winter for deer hunting season and they had two nightclubs up there. One was called Flamingo; one was called Paradise Club. . . . That was back in the days when it was about black and white bias, Jim Crow and stuff, and that was one of the few black summer resorts they had for blacks in the United States.

"Idlewild was a small, very small place, off the main highway, and a bunch of cabins, mobile homes, and there was a main cabin, a lot of sports, a beach and one club, the Flamingo, in those days we called it a budget club they'd book an emcee to put the show together and it would usually consist of four to five acts, and they'd have a chorus line, exotic dancers, maybe a novelty act, tap dancing and some comedy, and a small band. Whereas in the Paradise Club, they had the Las Vegas type revue and they would always feature or headline some name entertainment, like The Four Tops used to work there, but they were called the Four Aims . . . and Della Reese got her start up there and Johnny Ray, Frankie Laine."

Bill Pollack writing in the **Village Voice** (August 14, 1978), said of Jackie's club years, "His managers apparently believed that rock *'n* roll was a passing fad, and tried, unsuccessfully, to mold Jackie into a supper-club act. Bizarre interpretations of songs like *Danny Boy, Swing Low, Sweet Chariot,* and *You'll Never Walk Alone*, which turned up regularly on his albums, did much to erode the popularity he had achieved with his rock *'n* roll hits."

The supper club dilution caused many of Jackie's classic hits to be watered down into syrupy love ballads, which pleased the club patrons but soured rock *'n* roll fans. Nat had embarked Jackie down another road from which there was no turning back and by 1966 Brunswick was officially a one-artist label. Nat had placed all his eggs in one basket and it was full of holes. As Jackie's popularity began to wane toward the end of the decade, so did Brunswick's fortune. Nonetheless, undoubtedly due to a talent that just would not be quelled, Jackie sustained a slight comeback in the late sixties with three songs—*Baby Workout*, a strong rhythm and blues crossover dance tune which topped the R&B charts for three weeks in May 1963; *Whispers* in 1966, which made Billboard's #5 R&B and #11 pop charts; and *Higher and Higher* in 1967, now considered by at least one music critic to be the best single ever recorded.

Baby Workout, which was also the title of an album, was co-written by Alonzo Tucker and arranged by Gil Askey, who would go on to work with Diana Ross at Motown. Nat Tarnopol was so pleased with the success of *Baby Workout* that he kept Tucker on as Jackie's composer. Tucker, also from 1950s Detroit, had been a guitarist with The Royals. They went on to produce the hits *Baby Get It (And Don't Quit It)* and *Squeeze Her Tease Her (But Love Her)*, which was only a bottom-feeder on the charts. Tucker kept trying but most of his offerings were rejected by Jackie or his management for various reasons. Years later it was uncovered in an interview with Jackie that several of the songs from the ***Jackie Sings the Blues*** album credited to Tarnopol and his aunt, Lena Agree, were probably written by Tucker. Jackie is said to have loved Tucker and took him on the road often, sometimes as a driver.

Jackie also released some duets with Count Basie and LaVern Baker *(Think Twice and Please Don't Hurt Me)* during this time. An album with Count Basie called ***Manufacturers Of Soul*** was panned by critics who felt they were a stylistic mismatch, although many Jackie Wilson fans feel this album would be well received were it rereleased today. He also partnered with Linda Hopkins on singles *I Found Love, Say I Do, There's Nothing Like Love, When The Saints Go Marching In,* and *Yes Indeed,* and on the album ***Shake***

A Hand. They went on tour together as well, but despite these attempts his popularity continued to decline. Nat was forced to take action or risk losing Brunswick. Tommy Vastola introduced Tarnopol to a man named Carl Davis and, in one of the wisest moves of his career, he hired Davis as Brunswick's A&R director.

Davis had made a name for himself by producing hits for Major Lance, Walter Jackson, Gene Chandler and several other Chicago acts, but Jackie was the biggest star Davis had yet to deal with. Quoting from Chicago Soul, Davis tells how it all came about: "In August, 1966, I went to a disc jockey convention in New York, and that's when I met Nat Tarnopol relative to doing a production on Jackie Wilson. That's what we started off with, just a production deal between my company and Brunswick. And then after we did *Whispers* and the record was a huge success, then that's when Nat offered to bring me on as a staff person."

At this time, Len Schneider was president of Brunswick, and Nat was acting as vice president. Some of the success Jackie's recordings achieved under Davis had to do with the absorption of Brunswick by the Decca label, giving the former a boost in record distributions. Dick Jacobs, who was still working as arranger and orchestra director for Coral/Brunswick, said about the situation, "Whatever the title, Nat was running the company." When Brunswick was turned over in toto to Tarnopol, he made himself president with Davis as vice president.

Whispers was the first hit Jackie had for several years and it began a string of them for the next four thanks to the influence and care of Davis. When Jackie relocated his recording efforts to Chicago, he began working with a totally new group of artists—Sonny Sanders, Willie Henderson, and even soul writers such as Van McCoy and Eugene Record. Davis told Dave Hoekstra, a writer for Sun Times, 'When I began working with Jackie he was disenchanted with his management company because he wasn't getting the kind of material he wanted to do. I found him a beautiful person to work with, and he had a great deal of confidence in me. If he came into Chicago and I wasn't there, he wouldn't work until I got there. I knew what I was trying to do." Without question, Jackie scored his biggest hit with *(Your Love Keeps Lifting Me) Higher and Higher* in 1967, selling more than two million records. Bassist James Jamerson, Earl Van Dyke, and moonlighting Motown pianist Johnny Griffith aided Jackie's soaring and upbeat rendition and helped make it a hit.

Davis recalled that Jackie started out singing the tune like a soul ballad, but Davis encouraged him to pump it up and go with the percussion. "I would tell him that if he didn't want to sing it that way, I would put my voice on the record and sell millions of records."

Jackie's version differs somewhat. He told Norman Knight the song came about ". . . because they threw it away. They threw it in the garbage can. The guy that brought it in brought it in on a tape with a group singing and a little tinky-tinky guitar. No one could hear it but me. I could actually hear it. Well, I felt it was a church-type thing."

Relationships, whether business or personal, tend to erode when communication breaks down. Ironically, it was Jackie's biggest hit that finally initiated the deterioration of his relationship with Brunswick (although Harlean's relationship with Tarnopol must have been a mitigating factor, one the media would not have necessarily known about or reported).

According to Pruter, the conflict "between Wilson and Tarnopol was over the *Higher and Higher* and *I Get the Sweetest Feeling* albums. Said Davis, 'These albums did pretty good, a couple hundred thousand each. He felt they sold enough for him to get some money and he didn't. The problem continued, and after the *Beautiful Day* album was released, Jackie refused to go into the studio. It was a matter of principles and I really agreed with him. It was unfortunate, because for the remainder of his stay at the label we were not working on anything. We had to hold up until he felt he had caught up on his royalties and had something going.'"

While all these misunderstandings were working themselves out, or getting worse as the case may be, Jackie was sitting on the sidelines for the most part, except for a short stint in 1966 when he recorded two songs written by Raynoma Gordy's second husband, Ed Singleton: *She's All Right* and *Watch Out Baby*. Raynoma composed the string arrangements played by the New York Philharmonic. Of the result Raynoma wrote, "The songs scored well by us, and the work was a real shot in the arm. I was in my element. But all things being relative, it was hard not to compare a moderate hit of a star in decline with that ever-spreading comet trail of super hits coming out of Motown."

Jackie may have been idle but Brunswick was busy repackaging his old hits, including Jackie's 1961 album of Al Jolson hits which Brunswick retitled *Nowstalgia*. This album, originally released as BL 54100 and titled *You Ain't Heard Nothin' Yet*, contained a letter written by Jackie on the cover acknowledging his admiration for Al Jolson. Quoted here in part:

> To my way of thinking, the greatest entertainer of this or any other era is the late AL JOLSON. Even as a child, I can remember the thrill I always experienced whenever I hear him sing. I guess I have just about every recording he's ever made, and I rarely missed listening to him on radio. It's truly unfortunate that television couldn't have benefited by his talents. Regrettably, I've never had the privilege of seeing him perform in person. But even to this day, I am still one of his most avid fans.
>
> In no way is this album an attempt to imitate JOLSON'S style, nor is it an attempt to duplicate his incomparable way with a song. This is simply my humble tribute to the one man I admire most in this business. With the sincere hope that my contribution will in some way help keep the heritage of AL JOLSON alive through the great songs he left behind, let me here and now extend my deep appreciation to all those involved in making this album a proud moment for me. I

hope you like it!

Another complication in the morass seemed to be Brunswick's continued failure to grasp the ever-changing nature of music styles and public tastes. In its eagerness to bridge the white/black continuum, Brunswick resisted the growing appeal of soul music. Jackie's songs from the mid-sixties were considered ravers with gospel-like call-and-response vocals backed by big band arrangements that were becoming increasingly dated.

Jackie continued to perform from time to time around the country, prompting Pruter to include Chrissie Hynde's description of Jackie's stage show in the liner notes for Rhino Records' boxed set of Jackie's songs released in 1992. "I was fourteen when I went to see Jackie Wilson at the Akron Armory in 1966. He was topping the bill, which included Gorgeous George, Peg Leg Moffet, Pig Meat Markham, Aretha Franklin, and B. B. King.

"My girlfriend and I sat in the front row—the only whites in the audience. As his show reached a climax a member of his review pulled a girl out of the audience and took her to the foot of the stage where Jackie (who was at this point in the show lying down) kissed her. I had a feeling I would be next, and I was—that was my first kiss (a big wet one too). I'm not Catholic, but I imagine getting blessed by the Pope feels something like that. Oh, and what a singer!"

After Jackie's short rebirth during 1967 and 1968, he began to fade again toward the latter part of the sixties and early seventies with only one recording each year barely making the top 100 for

1969, 1970, and 1971. This dry spell was due in part to his es-
trangement from Brunswick, which had a concomitant effect on
the material provided, or in this case not provided, by Carl Davis.

As Jackie's professional life began to crumble around him, his
personal life collapsed as well. He and Harlean were divorced in
1969 after two years of marriage. Sometime before the divorce
was final he married Lynn Crochet, a cocktail waitress at a Mob-
owned club called the Black Knight in New Orleans. It was with
Lynn that Jackie had Thor and a daughter named Li-nie. Lynn described Jackie as a loving, doting father. "He sang to his six-week-
old daughter Li-nie the day of his collapse. He called twice every
day and sang to her. He was in Vegas when she was born. When he
got back from that trip he walked into the house and started singing
to her and she recognized his voice. Jackie and Thor would go
down to the railroad tracks and throw rocks and do simple things
he enjoyed."

Lynn and Jackie's marriage papers were never formally filed
and to this day the legality of their union is still being contested in
the courts. Nonetheless, both of Jackie's marriages were actively
producing new families during the same period of time during which
Jackie's oldest son, Jackie, Jr. was killed in a shooting accident.

Another tragic event that added great sadness to Jackie's tumul-
tuous life during the mid-1960s was the violent death of his close
friend, Sam Cooke. Sam and Jackie met in 1958 when Cooke was
headlining Irving Feld's "Biggest Show of Stars." The show con-
sisted of Sam and Jackie and eighteen other stars including the

Everly Brothers, Buddy Holly, Clyde McPhatter, LaVern Baker, and teen idols Frankie Avalon and Paul Anka. Feld was Alan Freed's competitor/nemesis and tried to get as many performances out of his stars as he possibly could, but the Stars tour was rife with racially discriminatory practices common to the era. In some states whites and blacks were not allowed to appear together on stage and audiences were segregated—whites into the good seats and blacks into the balcony. On the road, restaurants would serve the white performers in the group and ignore the black ones. Sometimes bigotry involved more than just going hungry.

Soloman Burke, quoted in Gerri Hirshey's **Nowhere to Run**, tells about a time in Shreveport, Louisiana, when Sam Cooke was on the way to New Orleans to perform in a show with B. B. King and Jerry Butler. They were staying in a small motel with a restaurant attached, but the establishment refused to serve the group because they were black. A waitress recognized Sam and offered to get his group their food and bring it to the back door of the hotel. But instead of food, a group of policemen arrived soon after she left and kidnapped them from the motel.

"They took us to the fire station," Soloman recalls, "and made us take off our clothes.

"They said, 'Now get your microphones, boys, and start singing.' They had us do the whole show. . . . And when we had finished the guy told us, 'Get in them stolen limousines, boys, and don't ever bring your band to Shreveport again.'"

The South was a dangerous place for blacks, and Jackie probably felt the need for some kind of protection. When asked whether they carried guns of any kind, Lamar Cochran replied, "Bang-Bang [Jackie's personal hairdresser] and I carried pistols. I had a .38 automatic. Jackie had a rifle in the back of the car, he had a 30/30. Jackie was a fascinating fella."

Daniel Wolff, in his biography entitled **You Send Me: The Life and Times of Sam Cooke**, told a similar tale involving racial hatred and its consequences that happened in February 1960. "Jackie Wilson, Little Willie John, Arthur Prysock, and Jesse Belvin were playing in Little Rock, Arkansas. It was a segregated Friday-night dance: the first audience Negro, the second crowd white. According to newspaper reports at the time, there was supposed to be a white band there, but they never showed up. Wilson played the first half of the gig but refused to go on for the white crowd. An ugly shouting scene followed, made uglier because Little Rock was still reeling from [a] school desegregation case. Cornered late on a Friday night in a city full of hate—the R&B stars nevertheless refused to go on and were finally ordered out of town at gunpoint. Prysock in his white Lincoln Continental, Wilson in his 1960 Cadillac, and Belvin in his '59 Caddy headed South to their next gig in Dallas.

"Wilson and Prysock had just passed Hope, Arkansas, when they started getting their first flats. While they'd been arguing in the dance hall, someone had slashed their tires. Belvin wasn't so lucky: five miles south of Hope, on Highway 67, his car went out into the passing lane, going eighty-five, and hit another vehicle head on.

Belvin, his wife, and the driver, Charles Shackleford, were all killed. No one ever proved that Jesse's tires had been cut, but the accident was a sign of the times. The rock & roll road was dangerous enough all on its own; add sudden national attention to a civil rights movement, and the singers became actors in a larger drama."

Frazier provides a possible explanation of why no one ever proved the tires had been cut: "I think one of the policemen cut his tires. He was passing a truck or something and the tire blew out, and that's how he had a head-on collision." (This contrasts somewhat with Etta James's version that Shackleford fell asleep at the wheel.)

That particular day was the only time Frazier had ever known Jackie to drive the car on a road trip. "We were coming into Mississippi and I had went to sleep, right? So, I'm laying in the front seat and I looked up and Jackie is driving. So, you know, like in Mississippi got these hills up and down, right. Weren't no expressway, right? It's up and down these hills, right? So I wake up, Jackie's hauling ass over these hills. So all of a sudden, here comes an old farmer . . . we come over this hill, right, and here come this old farmer easing out on the highway, you know what I'm talking 'bout? So, Jackie's doing 90, right? So the only way for him to go is to go in the ditch. That's why he went into the ditch and like, we had to get another car. And I think we got the car. . . 'cause we're going to Texas. We had to fly cause we're going to either Dallas or either Houston. I think he bought another car in either Dallas or either Houston. Yeah. That was too much for me, man. I woke up. That was at the same time [Jesse was killed] because he got killed that night, but we didn't hear nothing 'bout it until maybe like hours later."

It wasn't just the South. While Jackie was never a militant, he was actually banned from performing in Las Vegas for a time because he refused to be relegated to trailers in the back lot where blacks were given their dressing rooms. Jackie, who was really quite an egalitarian person when it came to racial matters, strode right through the front door like everyone else.

Nonetheless, because the Shreveport and Little Rock episodes were not isolated incidents, blacks tended to band together and keep to themselves, especially when touring in the South. Sam and Jackie had a lot in common and banded closely. They even shared the same woman. Jackie's valet, Frazier confirmed Sam had dated Harlean before Jackie did, around the time Jackie was with Billy Ward and the Dominoes.

Daniel Wolff wrote of Sam and Jackie's warm friendship: "On this tour [an R&B tour arranged by Dick Alen at Universal Attractions], Cooke co-headlined with Jackie Wilson, who had just come off his second pop hit, Lonely Teardrops and was pushing his third *That's Why (I Love You So)*. Sam and Jackie were always carrying on about who should be the headliner. It was a friendly competition: there's a rare film clip of Jackie bumping Sam offstage while he's lip-synching on a local TV show: the two men are all mock anger and banter. As the tour opened, 3,500 disk jockeys had just honored Wilson, along with Clyde McPhatter, for having the most records played on the air. To back this up, Wilson was an incredibly personable, acrobatic performer: a great mover known for his splits and spins. 'He'd be on the floor,' Alen recalls, 'he'd be up and down. He'd be taking his shirt off.'

"It was a seemingly impossible act to follow . . . [but] Wilson got to Cooke, made him move and abandon his teen-croon voice to shout a little, even laugh that gospel laugh."

Emcee Bill Murry confirmed Sam was the only person Jackie would share a headline with. "He and Sam Cooke were very close when it came to working together. The only person that he [Jackie] shared billing with that he had respect for was Sam Cooke. Jackie wouldn't share a headline with anybody else."

The two stars often orbited together and alternated the headliner spot depending on who was the most popular in any given town. Frazier said it was based strictly on money and it was a decision made by the promoter, although there are numerous instances where Jackie would not perform with others unless his name was above theirs on the marquee. With Sam, Jackie was different. "Yeah. They were great buddies," said Frazier of Jackie and Sam. "Sam was great, great. Yeah, he was great folk."

Gorgeous George's view of show business was that showmanship meant one upmanship and each succeeding act should outdo the last. Sam expressed his concern to George about following Jackie because of the way the women went crazy. Sometimes Sam would end the show and sometimes Jackie. When Jackie closed, according to George, all the women in the audience were up on the stage with him and it looked like the house was empty. While Sam was certainly a handsome man with a great voice, his stage act was more soulful and subdued as opposed to Jackie's wild splits, spins and similar theatrics. Sam did not have Jackie's boxing and athletic background so George advised him to up the wattage and take no prisoners. "No, he wasn't a dancer," says George.

"Remember now, Sam Cooke was a gospel singer. And you definitely couldn't dance to *Darling, You Send Me.* So, he peppered his show up with *Twistin'* and *Idle Wind*, tunes like that, man. *Cupid.* I mean Sam Cooke wasn't no pushover. He was a star.

"When Sam come on, he got them going, but not like Jackie. But Jackie Wilson was killing himself. One night I pulled [Sam] aside . . . I went to the dressing room. He was quiet and I said, man, you know the way you do when you used to kill those church folks, when you go to your knees, have women in bed and holler and sing; I said you got to do same way. I said pace the stage. Take your jacket and throw it cross your shoulder like Jackie. I said, Hey, you wearing this pretty stub jacket. Sam Cooke wore some bad stuff too. He wore some pretty stuff. He had his own style, custom made suits with the French cuffs and the German cuts with the wide lapels. So he started doing it. He started kicking behind, too. Then Jackie'd come on and he would make it hard for Jackie. Sam'd come on and Jackie would make it hard for him. It was a show, man."

Jackie and Sam spent many years touring together early in their careers. Though stars with well-known, handsome faces, they were still just two young black men driving through the rural south. Relating a story told to him by their chauffeur, Charles Cook, Wolff wrote about a time when Jackie and Sam were traveling together through Georgia in the same car and they spotted a group of black men dressed in white uniforms that contrasted starkly with the dark, red clay of the fields. It made a nice scene, until they got close enough to realize the group was being watched by mounted guards with shotguns resting in their laps. Then they saw the chains around their ankles and heard them singing.

"Sam heard the sound of the men working," wrote Daniel Wolff, "the call-and-response as the gang answered the lead, chanting in time to the long day's work—and started writing, there and then. After all, this was underneath all blues and gospel—as old as slavery, as old as the advent of black-skinned people on the continent. 'It was his idea,' Charles remembers, but all three men in the car helped with the song: struck not only by the scene outside the window, but by the very fact that it was outside—that the three of them somehow managed to be driving through Georgia in a new car, free to make the next gig, to write a song about chain gangs, while their brothers were locked together under the Georgia sun." *Chain Gang* was released by RCA in July of 1960. It reached #2 on the pop and R&B charts and sold more than one million copies.

Jackie included his own version of *Chain Gang* on his album with Count Basie, ***Manufacturers of Soul.*** It was also released as a single.

To Norman Knight Jackie said of Sam Cooke: "Ah, now you're

talking about a man that's a real stylist. Sam, to me . . . well, actually it's very well known that we were the best of friends and in fact, we were the only two at the time who would go out on tour together. We would never worry about top billing, we would just have me here one day and his name here the next day. This type thing. But, as far as singing and his style, I just don't think it will ever be equaled. It was God. His soul wept."

The mid-sixties were trying times for Jackie. In 1967 he was arrested in New York for possession of heroin, hypodermic needles, and two loaded guns. Sam Cooke was shot and killed in Los Angeles on December 11, 1964—the same year Freda Wilson filed for divorce; the same year Jackie was hung out a window in an effort to "encourage" him to renew his contract with Brunswick.

Chapter Nine

The Third Bang
My Heart Is Crying

*This time all of the people in the audience were screaming when he hit the floor. But when he went down the crowd thought it was part of his act and went on clapping, their hands moving rhythmically above them, stirring the dust motes highlighted in the spotlight shining from behind them at the man now lying on the stage. Slowly the clapping died along with the backup band's fading chords of **Lonely Teardrops.** Jackie did not get up.*

The last sound he heard was the crowd's collective gasp as Cornell Gunter bent over him and placed his lips on Jackies' mouth. "I can blink my eyes," he thought to himself, "but I can't move!" The pain in his chest was excruciating, much worse than the pain in his head where it had struck the floor. Then the lights began to dim. Is the show over? Pain flooded his brain but was soon replaced by a warm numbness and then blackness. The last sensation he had was a soft bumping as his consciousness bounced around inside his skull looking for a way out.

Gerri Hirshey in **Nowhere to Run: The Story of Soul Music,** probably described Jackie's life best: "Like Sam Cooke and Willie John, Wilson was fated to be an early soul comet, effectively burned out by the time singers like James Brown, Wilson Pickett, and Aretha Franklin were hitting their stride."

Now approaching forty, the hard years began to catch up with Jackie and leave their mark on his once youthful and smiling eyes. The press, eager to take pot shots at him when he became an easy target as his orbit slowed and degraded, reported several incidents of angry fans seeking revenge when he failed to show for performances. In Houston, Texas, when Fred Kibble was substituted at the last moment because Jackie did not show, an angry mob took $8,000 worth of vengeance on Jackie's Cadillac, slashing the tires and ripping out the antenna and telephone. It did not seem to matter to either the press or the mob that Jackie was in the hospital with the flu and a 105-degree temperature.

Ruth Brown in her autobiography recalled what was in store for other performers when Jackie didn't show. Brown, Bo Diddley, and Paul Williams were sharing a bill with Jackie at the Auditorium in Kansas City. Jackie had stayed behind with a woman he'd met at their prior night's gig in Atlanta, promising to catch up and be there on time for his performance. "There was no sign of him as Paul started the show," Brown wrote. "And when Bo followed him he did an extended act. He had to, for every time he left the stage Paul would say, 'Get back on and do another encore, Jackie ain't showed yet!'

"Eventually it was my turn to trawl through every song in my repertoire, saving 'Mama' for the finale. 'Still, no sign of Jackie. Keep goin'!' was the frantic message from Paul. As I was about to hit that tambourine for the eighth time, someone in the front of the huge crowd yelled out, 'Don't you sing that, not another damn time! Where's Jackie?' As the words echoed all over, a bottle whistled past my head, a sure sign they meant business."

When more bottles flew, the performers had to escape to their cars to avoid the angry crowd. Ruth Brown concludes: "Jackie? He ain't showed yet, and I've never returned to Kansas City since."

It's impossible to imagine or describe how traveling from town to town for months on end without a break could wear and tear on a psyche. Jackie, already deeply involved in alcohol and drugs, was exposed to angry fans, police brutality, the murder of his sixteen-year-old son, the deaths of two close friends, two divorces, the needs and demands of all his families, and repeated incidents of disgrace in the segregationist South. As his life suffered, so did his career.

After Tarnopol took control of Brunswick in 1970, few of Jackie's recordings were promoted as before. He and Davis and Eugene Record produced an album in 1969 entitled *Do Your Own Thing,* but it didn't fare well. The following year *This Love Is Real* made a showing on the R&B charts. Another Eugene Record composition, *You Got Me Walking*, was noteworthy but did not chart. Likewise, on the Las Vegas scene, Elvis was entering his white leather era. While still actively performing in a variety of venues, he was beginning to show the effects of too much everything. Elvis still has his faithful Colonel Parker; Jackie had Carl Davis.

Davis appears to have cared for Jackie even if his employer did not. In a desperate attempt to resurrect him, Davis hired songwriter Jeffrey Perry to compose a whole album of songs specifically for Jackie. The album **Beautiful Day** had one single, *Because of You*, that reached #45 on the R&B chart. It seemed no matter what Davis tried, Jackie's fans had deserted him. Ironically, it didn't seem to bother Jackie all that much. He and Davis were scheduled to record another album, **Nobody But You**. According to Davis, "Jackie was so excited . . . I was so happy to see him like this; finally, he seemed to have peace of mind. It was great working with him, and this album would have done the trick." It was apparent Davis, and not Tarnopol, was doing his best to prepare Jackie for the kind of comeback Neil Sedaka and Frankie Valli had recently achieved.

Then, just as it appeared Jackie was getting his life back together and was scheduled for a road trip and television variety show, the seven senior executives of Brunswick, including Nat Tarnopol, were indicted for taking $343,000 in kickbacks from retailers to whom they allegedly sold records below wholesale price; and for using part of the funds to pay off radio stations. Tarnopol was also indicted for wire fraud and conspiring to cheat the Internal Revenue Service.

In an interview recorded in Chicago Soul, Carl Davis described his astonishment at the indictment. "Nat was a very good executive and that's one of the reasons why I was confused, that he would do something like that. I really liked him and I considered him a good friend of mine, but then after the trial started, I realized that he wasn't as good a friend as I thought. He destroyed something that I had worked hard for all my life."

The remaining Brunswick staff and artists deserted the sinking ship, leaving Tarnopol left to turn the running lights on and off. Soon it became apparent there really wasn't much left to do and the Brunswick shipwreck slipped quietly beneath the waves.

None of Jackie's close associates knew what Jackie thought about this sad turn of events, or how it made him feel, although his wife Lynn believed by this time Jackie had grown to hate Nat Tarnopol. Most do attest that his normal modus operandi to escape his pressure cooker life was his down time on the long drives from show to show. He slept or listened to his favorite singers on the radio: Mario Lanza, Tony Bennett, and Frank Sinatra, paying his tolls with the little pieces of his soul he left along the highway.

Lamar Cochran, in his role as Jackie's road manager and valet, tells what it was like being on the road with Jackie. "He didn't like to fly unless he thought it was necessary. He was the kinda guy that couldn't come to the restaurant like normal people and eat. He'd have to have his food brought to him. Or, if we stopped somewhere at night on the way to another town, he wouldn't want to get out of the car. You'd have to go inside and get food for him, or somebody would cook something for him, like pork chops and things like this.

"God bless the dead again, his mother used to do that when we was leavin' Detroit. She would cook things like pork chops and biscuits and fried potatoes and so forth and stuff like that for him, and cake and stuff like that. This was our traveling food. Cake. He might give you a piece."

When it was time to move to the next booking, "Johnny Roberts would say, 'Lamar, you guys get packed up and hit the highway. We're goin' on into Miami tonight.' He'd tell Jackie to get ready. Johnny would say, 'Lamar, don't let him keep you here. If you do, you're fired.' I'd say, 'But hey!' He say, 'No, you're not fired. I'll take care of it. Jackie, I'll give you some money when we get to Miami.' Johnny would say, 'You got some money in your pocket, Lamar?' He'd give me maybe $500 to $600 and say, 'Here's some expense money.' I always had expense money because we had clothes to be cleaned. We always tried to get in town early in case we had to do something, get my car serviced. I always took care of these things.

"Jackie slept most of the time. Now he would wake up a lot of nights. The time that I would talk to him is when he and I would leave New York driving to Los Angeles and nobody in the car but him and I and the dogs. He had two champion poodles, Pete and Repeat. And then he had a little cocker spaniel named Poochie. We would drive and drive.

"In certain areas like Flagstaff, Arizona, for example, he wasn't afraid to get out at times. He didn't think people would recognize him or know him, but it wouldn't take but a minute and the minute he set his face in there somebody would say, 'Ain't that Jackie Wilson?' And there they come out of the kitchen and out of every place else, and they wanted his autograph and so forth, and there he go, sittin' right there he got to have a kiss. It don't make no difference where they are or who they are. I'd just sit there. I couldn't shoo 'em away because this is his public."

Lamar Cochran left Jackie's employ when it became frightfully obvious to him that Jackie had lost his sense of caring and compassion. "We were in Atlanta. . . and this young lady's husband shot her in the back. Little white girl. She had been up to see Jackie and he (the husband) didn't like it, and he killed her. She was about 20 or 21, somewhere like that, and Jackie had a young fella that was kinda workin' for him out there, kinda body guarding him a little bit at this club. Kid must have weighed 200 and some odd pounds. But the guy came up and wanted to see his wife and the bodyguard said, 'Mr. Wilson don't like people to be messin' with his ladies.' And the husband looked at him and said, 'You son of a bitch. That's my wife over there.' And she was trying to run across the parking lot and he shot her in the back three times, or it might have been five.

"It was something that just snapped me . . . the girl's mother was from up in Chattanooga or somewhere and she came down, and somebody had mentioned me to her and when she saw that I was black she didn't really want to talk to me. She was just torn to pieces. Her girlfriend had introduced the mother to me. She really didn't have anything she wanted to say to me because this has happened to her daughter and it was on account of a black man. I didn't want to press that issue.

"I left. I just didn't have no more desire to be around him. The man [Jackie] didn't show no compassion about what had happened. . . He got sick. He was in the doctor's office. One of Atlanta's disk jockey fellas saw him and was trying to talk to him and he just folded up and didn't want to talk to nobody . . . I imagine he felt bad [about the shooting] but the expression of compassion . . . there's a lot of different ways of showing how bad you feel about things when you don't really give a damn at all, so that makes a difference. So I just told him 'I'm through.'"

In Rock *'n* Roll Babylon, Gary Herman claimed Jackie was held as a material witness in the murder. Jackie had been playing for six days at the club where the twenty-one-year-old woman, named Karen Lynn Calloway, a former Playboy bunny and the mother of two children, worked as a waitress. Her husband claimed he shot Karen five times because she had become "infatuated" with Jackie.

Many people do not realize Jackie played outside the U.S. Frazier attests to their having traveled to the Virgin Islands, Jamaica, Barbados, British Guyana, and South America, and that the audiences went wild over him. According to Lynn Guidry, Jackie performed in the United Kingdom in 1972, and he also played to US military sites in Germany. The last time Frazier saw Jackie was sometime in the early 1970s when Jackie was booked with the Four Tops as a lounge act at the Flamingo Hotel in Las Vegas. Connie Francis was performing in the main room as a result of a "management decision," according to Frazier, but by this time Jackie's ego balloon was totally flat and he didn't seem to care that he was playing second string. "He really didn't care too much 'bout nothing I don't think," laments Frazier, " 'cause he didn't have nobody around that really cared about him."

Despite Jackie's decline in record sales, he was still able to command a $5,000 fee per show and his faithful manager, Nat Tarnopol, continued to take it from him until the bitter end. The end of Nat may have been very bitter indeed if Jackie had not retained a small part of his deepest soul. Frazier took matters into his own hands by ordering three hit men to kill Nat Tarnopol. In his own words, "I know one time we had been on a tour for about 90 days. So, at that time, Jackie would always send the money to Nat. So we got back to New York the last day of the tour and Jackie called Nat to send his mother some money or, you know, the kids some money, something like that. So, Nat tells him he didn't have nothing, you know, and Jackie got real upset about it. Okay? I'm saying to myself, Damn we just go on a fucking 90-day tour and at this time, like, black entertainers was 'bout the highest ones being paid. Like maybe, at least, it was like $5,000 a night. I mean that was big money for him. So I think Nat's excuse was that he took his percentage out, you know. So, anyway, I called a hit on Nat. I went uptown and I got Red Doan, I got Mile Leo and Trees. 'Cause I was, you know, I was really upset. So, Jackie kinda. . . he reneged that."

We can only speculate what fallout would have occurred during

Morris Levy's inevitable retaliation if the boys had carried out Frazier's hit. The incident is eerily reminiscent of a similar scene described in the early pages of **Elvis: What Happened?**, when Elvis asked the Memphis Mafia to call a hit on Mike Stone for stealing Priscilla from him. It was February 1973, and Elvis, progressing toward a drug-induced hysteria, was infuriated over losing his wife to a karate instructor. His bodyguards put him off repeatedly for several days until finally, thankfully, Elvis cooled down enough to realize the unreasonable nature of what he was asking them to do.

Jackie crooned his way through 54 charted singles, more than any other black singer in history. In **Hot Gospel**, author Clive Richardson writes, "Jackie Wilson said goodbye to the US Hot Hundred toward the end of 1973, when the crass, near-vaudeville *Sing a Little Song* struggled into the bottom of the soul listing. Brunswick Records and Wilson's manager, both with a mixed reputation in the business, were slow to promote his career, and internal conflicts contributed to his often uninspired records. Wilson relied upon rock revival shows to earn a living while reaping royalties from British reissues of his up-tempo soul hits."

By 1974, eight years after his last hit, *Higher and Higher*, Jackie was existing totally on the oldies circuit, rehashing old tunes for the audiences he had groomed himself the previous 20 years. He sang in Dick Clark's "Good Ol' Rock 'n Roll Revival" at the Las Vegas Hilton sharing the spotlight with Freddy Cannon, Cornell Gunter and the Coasters, live dancers, and nostalgic film clips. The show was a great success, due in small part perhaps to Elvis who showed up to watch with a bevy of friends and visit with Jackie backstage after the show.

Though on a much grander scale than Jackie, but with equally devastating consequences, Elvis was in decline health-wise, experiencing his own degrading orbit and succumbing to the stresses of touring and unrelenting fame. He was still tossing his sweat-stained scarves to sellout crowds, but it was obvious he was running on fumes. While insiders remained in awe of Elvis's ability to withstand a brutal touring schedule, Jackie had a similar constitution. It just gave out two years sooner.

In **The Elvis Encyclopedia**, author David Stanley said of Elvis' stamina, "If you've never been on the road, you don't know how hard it is, day after day. The farther down the road you get, the more tired you are, and there's no way to catch up, so you just keep going. To be fresh and up in every town you play takes a lot out of you. I swear Elvis was a machine. He was like that battery in the bunny: He'd just keep going."

David Stanley also quoted fellow Memphis Mafia cohort, Lamar Fike. "With all the controversy about Elvis' drug-taking and his physical condition toward the end of his life, people often forget what a tank he was. Nobody did what Elvis did in Las Vegas. Four weeks, seven days a week, two, sometime three shows a night. An awesome schedule. But he did it. Those of us who were there now understand that the man was working himself to death. Literally."

"I started out on the road in Guy Wilson's beat-up station wagon in Toccoa," writes James Brown in his autobiography, "moved up to some brand-new station wagon with Mr. Brantly, to a Cadillac and a bus, to commercial airliners, and then to three different private jets. It doesn't matter how you travel it, it's still the same road. It doesn't get easier when you get bigger; it gets harder. And it will kill you if you let it. There are lots of ways it can kill you: accidents, shooting, drugs. If you don't have the stamina you can even work yourself to death, like Jackie Wilson did. The road has killed a lot of good people: Jackie, Sam Cooke, Otis Redding, all those great entertainers."

Along with Fats Domino and Paul Gayten, Roy Brown was known for popularizing a mixture of New Orleans Dixieland boogie and ballads. Brown was a passionate performer with a wailing voice that greatly influenced B.B. King, Little Richard, and Jackie as well. Like Jackie, Brown had a heart attack on stage, and died in May 1981. Did the hard road described by James Brown claim yet another victim?

Writing in the Village Voice, Bill Pollack said that the last time he saw Jackie perform was in 1975 on a PBS special. Jackie, only forty-one, already looked paunchy and tired, ". . . but his voice was as strong as ever and his talent was fully intact."

According to Lynn Guidry, Jackie dried out completely for three years in the early 1970s and drank only Pepsi and smoked Viceroys. He had had a physical some time in June of 1975, and his doctors said they had not seen him in better shape for ten years.

On September 29, 1975, Dick Clark's oldies review arrived at the Latin Casino in Cherry Hill, New Jersey, after six weeks at the Las Vegas Thunderbird. "Jackie looks great," writes Newman and Kaltman, "as good as he's looked in years, after a long bout with alcoholism, drugs and other problems. The show goes on well, as act after act parades on and off, and Jackie takes the stage. Women are screaming, clamoring at his feet, and it's just like the old days. Exhilarated, he does one of his 'spins' as he worked into *Lonely Teardrops*, his traditional closing number. 'My heart is crying, crying,' says Jackie, and suddenly, he's on the floor, flat on his back. 'Get up,' hollers Dick Clark from the wings, 'that's a great act, but get up!'

"The first to realize it wasn't part of the act was Cornell Gunter, flamboyant lead of the Coasters. Realizing that something was very wrong, that Jackie had hit his head quite hard as he fell, Gunter immediately began mouth-to-mouth resuscitation while others screamed for assistance. A nurse came out of the audience to render cardiopulmonary resuscitation and the paramedics were called. (Although Jackie's brain damage later was ascribed to oxygen starvation during this period, Gunter insists that Jackie was breathing on his own; he also maintains that Jackie was at least partially conscious, responding with eye blinks when asked.) The ambulance arrived some 10 or 15 minutes later, taking Jackie to Cherry Hill Medical Center, the closest hospital in the area."

Lamar Cochran recalled, "The night of Jackie's heart attack in Cherry Hill, New Jersey, I was coming back from Los Angeles. I lived in Philadelphia at that time. As a matter of fact, his mother passed in Philadelphia (on October 16,1975 of a diabetic coma, slightly more than two weeks after Jackie's heart attack). . . When I heard he was at the Latin Casino after I got off the plane, I was coming back from the Academy Awards, I turned my radio on and the guy said Jackie Wilson is now appearing at the Latin Casino and the show is gonna start at such and such an hour. . . this is beautiful . . .I drove right across the bridge from the Philadelphia side into New York and went over there and the place was packed. When I got up there and parked my car and got inside they were taking him to the hospital.

"Well, like I said, I was comin' in. . . and you can always have a feelin' for a guy even though you know what his temperaments are. . . just to say hello, you know. The ironic part about it, you know, he was a wonderful fella. . . and we had a lot of great times and we stayed in the best places cross country. . . but life got to go on. . . and better standards are coming. That's what I figured when I was just gonna go see him and say 'Hey.' It was a blast while it lasted."

Several newspapers reported erroneously that Jackie had died, but in fact, he went into a coma as a result of oxygen starvation. A medic that was with Jackie on the way to Cherry Hill told Lynn Guidry they never should have shocked him, that he was not having a heart attack and they are the ones that caused the damage to him.

Lynn was not present at the time, she had just given birth to their little girl, Li-nie, and both of them were ill at the time. They sent

Jackie's mother's body to a medical school hospital in error. "It was a mess to straighten out. People just don't realize what I went through those first few weeks. It was horrible. And then Harlean came in and said she was his legal wife and all she wanted was his personal effects. She didn't give a damn about him. She hated him and he hated her (because) he caught her in bed with Nat Tarnopol." After lying comatose for three months, the medical staff attempted shock treatments on Jackie and injected stimulants into his heart. The treatments helped and Jackie stabilized. He awoke in January 1976 but had sustained extensive brain damage that left him wheelchair bound with limited motor functions and impaired speech. He attempted from time to time to communicate with those around him with sounds and eye blinks, but he spent the majority of his time staring into space with a vacuous expression, leaving those around him wondering what, if anything, he was thinking or feeling.

Said Lamar Cochran, "The damndest thing about it. . . every time I tried to contact him after that they would say he wasn't improving. He was withering away because he had never come out of it."

There was irony in the people who did or didn't come to see Jackie during this time. His wife Lynn stopped going to see him because Harlean was somehow able to prohibit her visits. Dick Jacobs, who professed to be a great friend, never visited Jackie at Cherry Hill because he didn't want to replace his image of the vibrant singer with the reality of the Jackie now living as a shell of his former self. This may be the justification many felt who also stayed away. It was obviously not a factor with Juanita Jones and did not prevent her from coming by to pay her respects to the man she shot so many years before.

Jackie hardly had time to warm his bed in the Cherry Hill Medical Center before allegations of negligence and malpractice began to swirl around him. According to Newman and Kaltman, "During the past 3-1/2 years, in a most vicious example of bureaucracy run amuck, Jackie has been bounced from place to place while arguments over his treatment (or lack thereof) abound. Literally since the moment he experienced the attack, one horror story after another has come to the forefront. There are allegations of indifference, misdiagnosis, mistreatment and even willful abuse. It has been alleged that an oxygen tank malfunctioned when Jackie first reached the hospital; that he was dropped out of a chair; that his wrist was broken in the process and never properly set in a cast; that he was left strapped in a chair, unattended, so close to a wall that he would repeatedly bang his head during convulsions; that, again, he was left unattended while a heat lamp had fallen on him and severely burned him; and so on."

Lynn Guidry provided some details about the later years of Jackie's life. He was, indeed, on the verge of making a new start right before his collapse in Camden. He had been scheduled to perform in his own television special but when tragedy struck, the show was given to Lola Falana. He had also approached Tommy Vastola about ending his contract with Tarnopol, and Johnny Roberts had been working on a deal with another record company for him. Roberts died in December, 1996.

Jackie Wilson's tremendous talent and dramatic approach to music were written about many times throughout his career, and there is not much that can be said that hasn't been said already in colorful fashion by those who were there while it was happening. He was called torrid, cool, crisp, athletic, articulate, energetic, the personification of soul, the epitome of natural greatness, a vocal and physical gymnast, a master of melisma, the most tragic figure of rhythm and blues.

And then he was called a vegetable.

Chapter Ten

Forever and A Day

From Jackie's point of view, if he had one, his frenetic life had wound down to a silent roar. We will never know to what extent his damaged mind was aware of the controversy and conflict swirling about him out of his earshot. First and foremost, it was quickly discovered that Jackie was broke, causing his wives to bicker over who was the real Mrs. Wilson and jockey for alimony money that did not exist. Ever-faithful Brunswick insisted Jackie owed them money and not the other way around. The IRS, who every US tax-payer knows is ever-infallible, claimed Jackie owed $300,000 in back taxes. All told, these claims tolled the death knoll for any spare change found lying around which could have been used for Jackie's immediate medical treatment and rehabilitation therapy.

Jackie hadn't had a hit record since *Higher and Higher* in 1967, but that he would be found bankrupt after almost twenty years of constant touring, 32 albums and 54 hit singles, estimated by one researcher to total $200 million in revenues, is baffling in the extreme. When the IRS looked to Brunswick for an accounting, they were informed Jackie owed them $150,000 in unreimbursed advances against royalties.

Most of what is known of Jackie's post-coma life was described in detail after sad detail by author Bill Pollack, who claims to have spent six months investigating Jackie's legal, medical, and financial problems. Pollack found, and graphically expounds upon, a strange conspiracy of events. For one, trade papers of the day said Jackie was more than broke, he was in deep debt at the time of his stroke. In addition to the amounts claimed by the IRS and Brunswick, Harlean had an outstanding judgment and warrants against him for child support and alimony which in effect had even prevented Jackie from setting foot in New York for some time prior to his collapse. The true and complete cause of his debt may never be completely understood, but Pollack poses some theories of his own.

Pollack intimated that the timing of Jackie's collapse was a rather fortuitous, highly coincidental event for Brunswick. Tarnopol and his henchmen had been indicted only three months before in the payola scandal, charged with the conspiracy outlined earlier. "According to the indictment," Pollack writes, "since these cash sales were not entered in the company books, the officials were guilty of tax evasion and of defrauding their own artists. If the charges against Brunswick were true, that explains where some of Jackie's money had gone—into the pockets of his manager and the executives of his record company."

With a criminal trial looming and Jackie being the only major artist Tarnopol had managed for the past twenty years, Jackie would have been the government's key witness to testify against him. Loyal to Tarnopol for so many years, Jackie's change of heart was well known. Their so-called brotherly relationship had become strained if not actually hostile. Pollack said, "His IRS debt and the legal problems with his wives would have given the government a potent means of encouraging his cooperation. But by the time the U.S. attorneys got around to interviewing him, Jackie was in a coma." Given what is known of the caliber of men who held Jackie's career in their hands, could this be a mere coincidence?

While Pollack falls short of alleging Tarnopol caused Jackie's collapse, it is indeed ironic that Jackie's stroke was also a stroke of good fortune for Tarnopol. Was it brought on by stress and/or anger? Or could it have been induced by an over-dose of drugs or other chemical means and no one thought to look? Since Jackie did not die there would have been no autopsy or inquisition. Or was it simply a matter of living life in the fast lane for too long with too many uppers and downers, minus one kidney and plus a bullet lodged in his spine? As Stallings says, "Jackie Wilson had always lived life on the edge." While intriguing and alarming, these questions and many others like them will probably never be answered.

Stallings also hinted at allegations of physical abuse if not downright mayhem. During the time Jackie was still comatose in Cherry Hill, he was discovered with two black eyes and a broken nose. The wooden arm of his wheelchair was found underneath his bed, leading to speculation that his injuries were the result of a beating. Were the Brunswick goons there to buy extra insurance Jackie would not miraculously recover in time to testify?

For six months after Jackie fell to the stage in Cherry Hill there was no legal guardian to make medical decisions and take responsibility for his affairs. He had lived and traveled with Lynn Crochet for a few years before marrying her in 1971, but Harlean arrived on the scene shortly after Jackie's stroke and claimed they had never actually been divorced, making his marriage to Lynn illegal. While the wives battled it out in the slow-moving court system, Jackie languished in limbo, robbed of his honeyed tenor voice and with no one to speak for him.

According to Pollack, "Because of the legal battle between the wives, time was lost in getting Jackie rehabilitated. In order to settle the dispute and get its bills paid, Cherry Hill Medical Center asked the court to intervene. In March 1976, a month and half after Jackie came out of his coma, Judge Vincent DiMartino of Camden County Court placed his affairs in the hands of an impartial third party, naming Edward N. Adourain, Jr., a Camden lawyer, as Jackie's legal guardian."

One month prior to Adourain's appointment, Tarnopol was convicted by a Newark jury of one count of conspiracy and 22 counts of mail fraud. In April 1976, one month after Adourain's appointment, Tarnopol was fined $10,000 and sentenced to three years in prison by Judge Frederick Lacey. Tarnopol did the expected and filed an appeal.

Meanwhile, as Pruter's research uncovered years later, people were still telling Jackie where to go, just like the old days. He writes, "After being adjudicated incompetent and no longer able to handle his affairs by the Camden Court of New Jersey, Jackie was moved to Penn Saulken Nursing Home for about five months. His guardian then had him moved to Morris Hall Rehabilitation Center in Lawrenceville, New Jersey, where he remained in therapy for nine months. He then went to Hannaman Hospital in Philadelphia for other procedures. Later, he was moved to Medford Leas Retirement Center, a retirement and rehabilitation facility where he underwent more therapy.

By all accounts, Adourain appears to have been a zealous advocate for Jackie's welfare. He knew the answer to who owed what to whom would be found in Brunswick's books, but they refused to allow him access, so he filed a lawsuit claiming breach of contract and demanded, among other things, a full accounting of Jackie's earnings, royalties, and advances. The complaint further alleged Brunswick owed Jackie over $1 million in royalties.

What was more important and of immediate concern to Adourain was finding money to pay for Jackie's rehabilitation. He fought in court and won a judgment against the Insurance Company of North America for $120,000 in past hospital bills. INA was also ordered to pay $119 a week in disability and continue workmen's compensation benefits. While certainly a victory, the rub was that workmen's compensation only provided limited coverage for therapy that will return an injured employee to his or her former job. Jackie's physicians were sure he would never sing again so INA balked at spending any money for this purpose. As much as the world would have wished otherwise, getting Jackie to sing again was not a priority. He faced many less noble hurdles, such as re-learning basic communication skills and how to feed himself.

Another ironic twist of fate came about when Adourain learned Jackie should have been covered under Blue Cross/Blue Shield through his union's pension and welfare plan from the beginning. Pollack notes, "Under Section 34 of the AFTRA (American Federation of Television and Radio Artists) Pension and Welfare Clause, which also includes all recording contracts, an artist is eligible for Blue Cross/Blue Shield if he earns $1,000 a year or more. Wilson had been working on an album, *Nobody But You,* for three months before his collapse, and had put in over 24 hours in the studio. Since the rate for studio time is $81.50 an hour, Wilson should have easily met the AFTRA's requirement."

Brunswick easily circumnavigated this loophole by again sticking to their claim that Jackie owed them $150,000, and so they did not pay him any salary for 1975. When Cherry Hill contacted AFTRA in an attempt to get its bill paid, they were told Jackie was not eligible. Adourain argued that it mattered not whether Jackie owed money to his employer, it mattered that he met his contract obligations, that he came and he sang, and Brunswick was bound, by law, to contribute to his pension fund for the time Jackie worked.

It seems hardly fair to fault Adourain for discovering all this too late, but once the INA's benefits were set in place and coverage denied for Jackie's rehabilitation, Blue Cross/Blue Shield could not be required to pick up those payments.

With the exceptions of Adourain, who was performing his services on Jackie's behalf for a fee, and Lynn Guidry, who states, "If I had been in charge, if I had been his guardian, a lot of things would have been done differently. . . . He probably would have been rehabilitated to where he could at least talk."

There is only one person involved in Jackie's post-stroke life that seemed to have only his best interests at heart. Joyce Greenberg McRae, whose only relationship to Jackie was that of a friend, moved from her home in Chicago to look after his care and treatment. There was no financial benefit to her, she stood to gain nothing and, in fact, would lose almost everything in her fight to see that Jackie received nothing more or less than the care he deserved. If there is a hero in this story, it has to be Joyce McRae.

Jackie's condition was labeled "semi-comatose" when McRae arrived in New Jersey shortly after Adourain had been appointed Jackie's guardian. She described his condition as changing daily; some days he seemed lucid and aware, responding to people, conversations, and activities around him. Other days he seemed to have retreated into a silent void. As she continued to monitor his situation, she saw he was receiving no rehabilitation and she knew she had to remain there until she could secure some kind of useful therapy for him. Pollack quotes her as stating, "I felt he needed to have someone without any self-serving motives near him to look out for his interests."

McRae and Adourain worked together at first to arrange testing by physical therapist Dr. James Richardson to determine Jackie's capacity for rehabilitation. Richardson began treating Jackie with PNT, proprioceptive neuromuscular therapy, to revitalize and develop neuro-pathways in the brain. Richardson also recommended a treatment called "patterning" in which the patient learns to crawl like a baby again, which stimulates the primal pathways in the brain that coordinate the muscles of the arms and legs.

The patterning therapy began a new round of controversy in Jackie's medical treatment. Perhaps because it is a very simple treatment easily learned and administered by lay people, it was frowned upon by some of the medical community. In June, 1976, INA called in Dr. William J. Erdman of the University of Pennsylvania to determine if Jackie was a candidate for therapy. Erdman's conclusion was that Jackie was untreatable and any attempts at rehabilitation were fruitless. This was the only excuse INA needed to stop funding Richardson's treatment procedures.

Pollack reports, "Between March 30 and May 6, 1977 Jackie was tested at Hahnemann Hospital in Philadelphia to find out whether surgery might help his condition. The hospital performed a brain scan on Wilson, and concluded that surgery would not be of value. Dr. Wilson W. Oaks's discharge summary said that Jackie Wilson's potential for rehabilitation was limited, but it did recommend that Wilson be given the opportunity to avail himself of some rehab program on a continuing basis. . . . 'We made every effort to do more than just passive range of motion here,' the summary said.

'We had him on the tilt table and [gave him] physiotherapy trying to get him to stand. It was difficult to have him standing at this time but perhaps a more aggressive physical therapy approach with some braces might be able to accomplish this goal.' For some unknown reason, no one paid any attention to Dr. Oaks's opinion."

Jackie's guardianship matters were taking too much time away from Adourain's law practice and in February, 1977, he asked the court to grant him leave to withdraw. McRae petitioned the court requesting she be allowed to serve as guardian and care for Jackie in her home, but since she was not an attorney or officer of the court, Judge DiMartino determined she could not be held sufficiently accountable for carrying out the court's wishes. In April, 1977, the court appointed Camden attorney Wayne R. Bryant in Adourain's stead.

Bryant did not appreciate what he felt to be McRae's meddling and second guessing, and they were at odds from the outset. McRae claimed Bryant threatened to have her arrested on one occasion. McRae proved to be a conscientious defender of Jackie's health concerns, but once her guardianship petition was turned down, the hospital staff became disinclined to give consideration to her suggestions and criticisms.

McRae and Bryant's antagonistic relationship turned decidedly hostile when Bryant suspended Jackie's speech therapy without taking into consideration the therapist's report that there was a chance Jackie might regain some language skills. INA was picking up only half of Jackie's room rate at Medford Leas and Jackie's estate was paying the remaining half. Bryant stopped the speech therapy when the balance of the estate reached $10,000. McRae was furious and began paying for the therapy from her own pocket. Like others before her, McRae kept getting the sensation that mysterious, sinister forces were at work behind the scenes. "This has been a consistent pattern in Jackie's health care," she said, "and I don't know how to explain it. But as soon as Jackie makes any kind of progress, something always seems to happen to cut off this therapy and allow him to regress."

McRae and Bryant continued to butt heads over what was best for Jackie. After McRae voiced her concerns to local newspapers in Philadelphia and South Jersey, Bryant obtained a court order preventing her from visiting Jackie in Medford Leas and again stopping the speech therapy she had been paying for.

It is not clear why Bryant fought so hard against McRae to the detriment of Jackie or why the court allowed him to prevail. Nurses and doctors from Medford offered testimony that McRae had a "calming" effect on Jackie and that he had formed "a definite emotional attachment" to her.

Based on these claims, McRae persuaded the court to allow her to see Jackie for two hours every day. It took McRae somewhat longer to get the speech therapy restarted and by the time Jackie visited the therapist, he had lost whatever progress he had made previously. The therapist revised her prior findings and stated Jackie's vocal processes were beyond repair. Jackie never received any speech therapy after this time and the two thousand dollars that McRae had raised from a record company to pay for it was never used.

McRae finally lost her patience. According to Pollack, "Bryant's actions prompted McRae to file a lawsuit in Camden County Court asking that he be removed as guardian for allegedly failing to carry out the court's directive to 'do all things reasonable, necessary and proper to attempt the rehabilitation of Jackie Wilson to whatever degree or extent possible.' She contended that Jackie had regressed badly since Bryant took over as guardian. In addition, McRae again asked the court to name her Wilson's guardian, so that she could care for him in her home."

As a result of mounting legal expenses, including those incurred in defending herself against counter charges of interference filed by Bryant, McRae ran out of money and returned to Chicago. Shortly thereafter, Bryant requested that he be allowed to resign as guardian. On April 14, 1978, ruling against guardianship petitioners Joyce McRae and Tony Wilson, Jackie's son by a previous marriage, Judge Ellen Talbot named Harlean Wilson guardian in place of Bryant. Harlean's lawyer, John T. Mulkerin, was appointed Jackie's legal representative. Together, they made public statements to the effect that they would spend whatever money was necessary to rehabilitate Jackie no matter what the chances were for success and no matter what the cost. There was only the small matter of the fact that there was no money whatsoever. We are left wondering where Harlean's support was during McRae's selfless and singular battle against bureaucracy and whatever other forces may have been aligned against her success.

Meanwhile, other musicians watched in amazement and horror to what was happening to the much revered Mr. Excitement. Many of them must have looked inward and saw that it could very well happen to them. While lawyers and wives wrestled off stage, they held benefit concerts to raise funds for Jackie's care. The Spinners raised $60,000 in a benefit concert in October of 1976. Barry White contributed $10,000, Ben Vereen established a fund to raise additional monies, and Elvis Presley sent Jackie's wife a check for $30,000. It should surprise no one that much of the money raised for Jackie's benefit went to outstanding lawyers' bills and that there was none left to continue Adourain's litigation against Brunswick to reveal their accounting records. In November, 1977, the Third Circuit Court of Appeals overturned Nat Tarnopol's convictions and remanded the case for retrial. When the parties returned to the courtroom in May, 1978, the government's case fell apart because, due in part to his aborted speech therapy, Jackie had no voice whatsoever, and there was no one left able to offer direct testimony of Brunswick's alleged fraud against their artists.

On July 4, 1977 the following blurb appeared in the Chatter department of **People** magazine: "Twenty-one months after he collapsed onstage at the Latin Casino . . . with a massive heart attack and resulting brain damage, R&B singer Jackie *(Higher and Higher)* Wilson's plight is sadder than ever. Bedridden in a nursing home in Medford, New Jersey, he communicates by blinking his eyes and eats baby food. Yet the IRS is suing him for $234,000 in back taxes, and two women—each claiming to be his wife—are fighting over his estate. Further, a friend who cares for him says she is 'disgusted and disheartened' by the short memory of Jackie's friends and fans. On his 43rd birthday last month, Wilson (who once cut seven gold records) received six cards."

This news item is somewhat misleading in that John Mulkerin admitted elsewhere that he was driving around with a bag full of mail for Jackie in the trunk of his car. Ralph Newman and Alan Kaltman visited Medford Leas Retirement Home in July, 1977 and interviewed McRae in Jackie's presence. During the interview Jackie made eye movements and grunts, which Joyce interpreted for the authors. About the sad state of Jackie's affairs, Newman and Kaltman wrote: "The ultimate tragedy, however, has got to be the incredible apathy. It has been said before but obviously bears repeating: what is wrong with a society that reveres its performers as we do, that elevates them to the absolute heights when we need them, and then throws them away, like so much litter on a whim?"

Pollack quoted WDAS (Philadelphia) disk jockey George Woods in 1978 on Jackie's post-stroke condition: "In the early 1960s Jackie was number one—there was nobody bigger. He was pure electricity on stage, one of the greatest performers that ever lived. I really can't understand why he's in the position he's in today. It's sad. I always thought he was more loved than that. All those people he helped—you wonder where they are now.

"But you know how it is. If they can exploit you, they're gonna do it. This is the way our business is—everybody does it. They suck the blood from you and then leave you alone. . . .I think Jackie's a victim of being used by the wrong people."

The burning question remains—had Jackie been able to testify against those who wronged him, would he have?

Chapter Eleven

Alone at Last

Even as Jackie languished at Medford Leas Retirement Community, he continued to be recognized by the world as a great artist. Irish songwriter Van Morrison often claimed Jackie was a great influence and wrote *Jackie Wilson Said (I'm in Heaven When You Smile)*. The Commodores' *Nightshift*, a tribute to both Jackie and Marvin Gaye, reached #5 on the transatlantic charts in 1985. *Reet Petite* was rereleased in the UK and reached #1 during Christmas week in 1986. Rita Coolidge, Shakin' Stevens, and many others rerecorded some of his hits, and compilations of his recordings were reissued by Kent, Epic, and Columbia Special Products labels.

After eight years of living in a world without music and meaning, Jackie was admitted to Burlington County Memorial Hospital in Mount Holly, New Jersey, on January 8, 1984, which would have marked Elvis' 49th birthday. Death arrived at Jackie's door January 21st at the age of 49, but it was anticlimactic and barely noticed outside his family and close friends. *A New York Times* obituary stated that Jackie's legal guardian, John P. Mulkerin, had visited Jackie six weeks prior to his death. "He was in a semi-co-matose state," Mr. Mulkerin said. "He was 100 percent dependent on care."

Probably for the simple reason they could, Jackie's family re-quested that the hospital not release his cause of death, although *Jet* magazine listed it as pneumonia, and Lynn Guidry claimed the death certificate stated he died of strangulation.

Fifteen hundred mourners attended Jackie's memorial service at the Russell Street Baptist Church, including the Four Tops and the Spinners. Photos in the February 13, 1984, *Jet* coverage of the fu-neral show Harlean, son John, and John Mulkerin, still Jackie's legal guardian. Also present were Jackie's children LaShawn, Jacqueline Denice, Thor (the former hammer throwing babe from Marietta, Georgia), Anthony, his grandson, Norbert Pennell, Jr., and sister Joyce Collins.

Collins told the *Jet* reporter her brother's fancy footwork on-stage was adapted from the moves he had used in the ring. "'My brother wasn't a dancer. Actually, those were a lot of boxing steps he incorporated into his act." She added, 'I've seen a lot of enter-tainers, but I have to say he was the greatest."

Also in an interview with *Jet,* Reverend Dr. Anthony Campbell, who held the service at his church, is quoted poignantly as saying, "Most of us live beyond having the strength to die. I think Jackie, just realizing he would never be dancing, singing and swirling, just turned in on himself." When cries arose from the mourners,

Campbell told them, "You should cry when a baby is born. We're here to celebrate a life. We cannot celebrate a life like Jackie Wilson's without joy."

James Brown, who could not attend the funeral due to singing engagements on the West Coast, sent a flower arrangement in the shape of a record with a photo of Jackie and the words "Lonely Teardrops" inscribed with gold letters. On the card accompanying the flowers, he wrote: "There will never be another like this soul brother."

Other observations on the funeral were made by Frank Joice and printed in **Rock & Roll Confidential**. Joice wrote, "There were many teardrops shed in Detroit's Russell Street Baptist Church on January 28, 1984, but they certainly weren't lonely ones. On a cold but brilliantly sunny Saturday afternoon, more than 2,000 mourners crammed into the balcony, basement, aisles, and sidewalks of the church for the funeral of Jackie Wilson.

"'Some of you came to see. Some of you came to be seen. Some of you were there when Jackie needed you. Some of you weren't,' said the Rev. Dr. Anthony Campbell in his eulogy." Joice described the ceremony as joyous and high-spirited due to the singing of the Russell Street Baptist Church's Celestial Choir. It was from their sounds that Jackie's voice, energy, and spirit sprang many years before.

Joice further quoted Reverend Campbell as saying, "I can't find Jackie Wilson in his songs." Campbell explained how he used to sneak out of his house at night as a young man to watch Jackie perform, and that while Jackie's songs were sometimes silly and frivolous, it was a marvel at how he put them together.

Levi Stubbs called Jackie "street people," meaning those who never become bigger than real people. "If there was a genuinely sad note at the funeral," Joice wrote, "it came when the Rev. Campbell asked all the performers and entertainers in the audience to stand. Not only Levi Stubbs but the rest of the Four Tops rose to their feet, as did all the Spinners. In all, nearly 200 people stood. Not a single one was white. That, too, is cause for grief." Lynn Guidry, who is white, was present at the funeral along with other whites. "When he died Harlean sent word to me, I could not go to the funeral but that I could send the kids. I told her unless she met me with an injunction I was comin'."

In a personal interview with the author, Reverend Campbell, gave his version of some of the unusual occurrences at Jackie's funeral. "She [Harlean] had fought off all the people who had tried to exploit him and at the funeral there were people trying to take pictures in the casket. There was one guy who was a Jackie Wilson look-alike who claimed to be Jackie's illegitimate son. One lady showed up in a wedding dress—at the funeral—to marry Jackie. It was bizarre."

Lynn Guidry was unhappy about the choice of pallbearers, saying, "Jackie fired August Sims because all their years together he was really working for Nat Tarnopol and not Jackie. He was a pallbearer at the funeral. Jackie would not have wanted that." She added that before the funeral, Jackie's body had been placed in a Detroit mortuary where winos hung out in front. The next day they moved him to a church. "He would not have wanted an open casket. I had it closed but it was too late. The press had already taken pictures."

"Well, we protected her," says Campbell of Harlean, "and we assigned officers to protect her and when the phonies and the royal flushes tried to come in and exploit, we corralled them to the side. It was a monster funeral. My church seats about 1100, and we had about 2000 in there that night. Later on, she was a featured guest at Jackie's family affair, which is held in Atlanta most every August. She ended up being roommates with an old girlfriend of mine, so I kind of followed her and would send greetings to her every year. But I have not seen her since Jackie's funeral."

The controversy did not stop when Jackie died. In fact, it followed him to his grave and beyond, and there was even great public debate about his final resting place. Writer Ken Settle in his July 17, 1987, *Goldmine* article claimed Jackie was buried in a grave site marked only as #117, with his name written on a wooden stake in felt pen. Settle further claims this diminutive marker was donated as a gesture of respect from music photographer, Bob Alford, intimating that had Alford not provided it, Jackie's grave would not have been marked at all.

Settle's assertions on face value are hard to believe given the well-publicized memorial services and large crowd on hand to pay their respects, but in fact Reverend Campbell's statement provides some insight. "He was buried in essentially the family plot. It was not a pauper's grave. The reason somebody might think it was that it was an older cemetery, rather not well cared for. He is interred with a big monument over him. He was buried like a prince. And again, I think that people going out to the cemetery expected something like, you know, Hollywood Roselawn or something. What they saw was a hard scrabble cemetery with a regular tombstone, ill-kept.

"You know, that cemetery has been a black cemetery for a hundred years. But he's buried with his mother out there . . . in essentially a family plot. And by the way, the lawyer, after the funeral was over, sent the church a check for $700 or $800 for the residual of Jackie's estate. He said, 'You know, I protected him the best I could, we buried him properly and I'm sending the remainder of his estate to the church as a donation.' Now that doesn't say he was buried in a GI issued box with a welfare check tombstone kind of thing."

In **Rage to Survive,** Etta James wrote, "While Jackie lay in a coma after his stroke in the mid-seventies I used to call and ask about him all the time. I also made several trips to New Jersey to be close to him, but I could never enter the room he was in. I could not face seeing what had been such a fine, vital man in such a hopeless condition. There had been so much in the tabloids of him laying there, muscles wasted and slowly fading away, and it hurt me so bad. When they went through the farce of fundraising to place a headstone on his grave, I had to speak out in disgust. A headstone? How much did that cost? Why couldn't his record company, who'd no doubt made millions off him, pay for it?"

Settle reported that music newsletter publisher Jack "The Rapper" Gibson initiated a drive to raise funds for a grave marker in January of 1987, a full three years after Jackie was buried. Gibson started the drive with $500 of his own money and received funds totaling $18,000, including some from international contributors.

On June 9, 1987, an unseasonably cool summer day, more than 150 people gathered again in Jackie's memory. It would have been Jackie's 53rd birthday. This time it was at Westlawn Cemetery in Wayne, Michigan, for the dedication of a granite and brass mausoleum, the final resting place for Jackie and his mother, Eliza Lee. The tomb was inscribed with the words, "No More Lonely Teardrops." A carved granite meditation bench bearing the words "Jackie—The Complete Entertainer" was positioned in front of the headstone.

Included in the attendees were local civic leaders and radio personalities. LaBaron Taylor, vice president of CBS Records, was present, and a city councilman for Highland Park named Linsey Porter announced that the council had voted to rename a street "Jackie Wilson Drive."

Settle reports that Gibson displayed "obvious pride and affection." Speaking to those gathered, he said, "If Jackie Wilson had not blazed upon our leisure time world like he did, and left his mark in so many entertainers, it's very possible that a lot of us today would have journeyed down different paths. Thank you personally, Jackie. Thank you for touching the Rapper's life. And thank you for the many entertainers that adopted your style. You're truly a legend we will not forget. Here, your final resting place with your mother will be the shining beacon for all to see long after we have been forgotten."

Others who spoke, like Jackie's sanctimonious road manager, August Sims, were saddened by the absence of the many people Jackie had helped throughout his career. "I'm happy that you people came out," Sims said. "I hope that everybody across the country will see this. All the other entertainers that Jackie had on his shows. I don't see many of them here."

Nonetheless, many people and fans did attend the celebration held that evening in Detroit at the Latin Quarter Club, including the Floaters, the Spinners, and boxing great Muhammad Ali.

Jackie was inducted into the Rock and Roll Hall of Fame in January, 1987, during its second annual ceremony at the Waldorf Astoria Hotel in New York City. In her autobiography Ruth Brown talked about a sad but telling scene that occurred when Joyce McRae attended the ceremony with two of Jackie Wilson's daughters. Joyce had been the wife and manager of Sam Moore, one-half of the Sam and Dave team. She'd been involved with Jackie in the late 1960s and, according to Brown, was "well aware of the rocky relation-ship that existed towards the end with his last official wife, Harlene (sic). As head of the Hall of Fame, Ahmet [Ertegun] had decreed that Harlene and the son she claimed was Jackie's—a claim dis-puted in some quarters—be the sole family members allowed to attend his posthumous induction. This was regarded by many as arrogance on the grand scale, flying in the face as it did of a court decision in Georgia that acknowledged the legal status of two daughters by his common-law wife."

Joyce was standing outside the Waldorf trying to smuggle the daughters into the ceremony. Ruth says: "I took one look at them and my heart melted. One was nine, the other thirteen and a polio victim, and both, I swear to God, were so obviously Jackie's kids no one would have denied them." The girls were admitted and on their way inside Brown told them, "Your dad was wonderful and a dear, dear friend."

"All went well, right up until a few minutes before Jackie's induction. At that point a couple of six-and-a-half-foot-tall goons appeared. 'The kids are gonna have to leave,' they announced. 'Only Jackie Wilson's wife and son are involved in the presentation.'" The girls pleaded to be allowed to remain, but they were taken from the room in tears.

According to Marc Eliot in **The Money Behind the Music**, Ahmet Ertegun put up $1.5 million to establish the Rhythm and Blues Foundation in 1988. The organization's purpose is to locate lost, stolen, or "misappropriated" royalties owed to some of the rhythm and blues performers from years ago.

Also appalled by the tragedy of Jackie's life and death, Joey Dee and a large group of musicians and deejays formed another organization, the Starlight Starbright Foundation, to raise money for a home for destitute rock and rollers. Eliot writes, "The purpose of the organization is to help those whose careers failed to provide them with enough money to live out their final days in dignity. For the rockers with no pensions, no social security, out of sight, out of money, and finally out of their minds, it was never only a song."

There are still a number of issues pending in the courts, particularly concerning the various legalities of Jackie's marriages and the rights of his children. Although a 72-song compilation of his recordings was released under the Rhino Records label in 1992, the ownership of much of his work remains at issue. As to the rights to his songs, Reverend Campbell stated, "Jackie had enough money to be buried decently, but unfortunately the title to his records and his songs and what not had lapsed and been stolen and otherwise abused. Some of them had been sold off by his son, who is an alcoholic, and some were taken by various women claiming to be wives. . . . I think if you asked Harlean that question directly, she would tell you she doesn't (hold any rights). At Jackie's death, the lawyer told me he had no rights to any of his music; it had all been lost or stolen. This is, in fact, partially substantiated. Bill Holland reporting in the July 19, 1997, Billboard stated an archivist reported sections of master tapes of Jackie Wilson's and Buddy Holly's recordings were "cut right out of the 3-track masters' reel."

Reverend Campbell continued, "But I am sure that someone has some kind of title and I am sure it would be hard to prove otherwise. But, you know, this happens a great deal. Till Berry Gordy came up with his scheme, routinely black artists, be it Jellyroll Morton, anybody else, would give them away for a pittance, especially in the gospel and religious field, especially [in] places like

Chicago, Detroit, and Philadelphia. I'd be very, very surprised if he had title to anything."

Don Wailer wrote in his obituary on Jackie in the January 29, 1984, Los Angeles Times: "Wilson knocked out audiences uptown (at the Apollo) and downtown (at the Copacabana) alike with his dazzling footwork and incredible stamina. Contemporaries remember him doing a back-flip, tearing off his jacket, and coming up twirling it around his head all in one fluid motion—just in time to sing the next line, of course. There's precious little live footage of Wilson in existence, although rumors of home movies featuring 'Mr. Excitement' in action have whetted collectors' appetites for years." Including an especially enticing CD. Lamar Cochran said, "LaVern Baker was out on the road with us for a while. She and Jackie were real close, if you know what I mean.

"They'd be in hotels together but she didn't travel with us in the car. They recorded an X-rated version of 'Think Twice' that can be found on a bootleg CD."

Reverend Campbell also reflected upon what might have become of memorabilia, and Jackie's personal items that might have become collectors' items since his death. It got him thinking in particular about the program from the Russell Street Baptist Church funeral. "I was pastor of the church from '82 to '87. I left in '87 and I came back in '93 at their request. When I left there was a copy of the funeral program. There was an original plate, because we did 2500 copies of the funeral program and it became a collector's item almost immediately. When I came back, people had tried to buy the plates for the very reason we're discussing, 'cause it was an extremely well done funeral program with photographs. All of that material was destroyed. I mean it was not sold; it was destroyed between the time of my leaving and coming back. So I am 100% certain that there's nothing by way of memorabilia of him, the family, or anything else around the church."

Gorgeous George still owns some of Jackie's suits. He is particularly proud of a buckskin leather suit Jackie wore during an impromptu concert before a crowd of 600 in a club in Forsyth, Georgia. George also rescued two pieces of his jewelry, bracelet and a ring, from a pawn shop. The ring had his initials and an inscription from his manager on the inside.

You would have to be living on another planet to be unaware of the tremendous glut of Elvis Presley memorabilia. Elvis died August 16, 1977, six and one half years before Jackie. Elvis sold 45 million records and starred in 33 films, yet at the time of his death his estate was also shockingly small, valued at $4.5 million.

The assets, in the form of Elvis Presley Enterprises (EPE), were left in trust to his daughter, Lisa Marie, with her mother Priscilla taking over as trustee in 1979. Years of legal battles followed as EPE tried to regain control of the Elvis image to prevent the endless tide of trinkets and memorabilia from flooding the market and thereby lessening the marketable value of the dead rock and roll star. Tenacious and successful, EPE was turned over to Lisa Marie, but with Priscilla still in charge. It is now worth an estimated $200 million.

It matters not whether you sell your soul to the devil, or to some more earth-bound marketing tycoon, you forfeit it nonetheless at Saint Peter's gate. Let's hope the Black Elvis and the White Elvis are gyrating, swinging, and singing up a storm in rock and roll heaven.

Epilogue

Am I the Man?. . . Yes, You're the Man

"I was born and raised in Detroit. My mama did some singing. I never studied music. Didn't like instruments. But I sang in church— Mother Bradley's Church—spirituals and gospel. I liked that. Gave me good feelings."

—Jackie Wilson

"If the *Academy of Television Arts and Sciences* ever asks me for highlights from the fifties that represent American Bandstand at its best, I would have to start by selecting a clip of Jackie Wilson. He was called Mr. Excitement and with good reason. Wilson was one of the most dynamic performers I've ever seen, and he was a strong influence on Elvis Presley, and later on, Michael Jackson and Prince, as well as many other artists. He had been a Golden Gloves boxer and was a fantastic dancer. Jackie made his Bandstand debut on October 4, 1957, singing his very first single, *Reet Petite,* co-written by Berry Gordy, who later started Motown Records. Jackie Wilson is gone but his work stands up to this day."

Dick Clark (in)
<u>Dick Clark's American Bandstand</u>

"Here's young Jackie Wilson out of Detroit, now living in Harlem. I suppose there's no performer of his race who is as well beloved as Jackie Wilson by his own people and by record fans everywhere. Since 1957, his records have sold six millions copies, and I'm going to ask him tonight first to sing two of his great hit records—*To Be Loved* and *Lonely Teardrops*. Here is— making his first appearance on television—Jackie Wilson! So I want a tremendous applause."

[Later in the show Jackie came back on to sing *Alone at Last*. Ed called him over to his side and said, "Now, ladies and gentlemen, that's the first of many appearances he's going to make on our stage if I have to drag him on here."]

Ed Sullivan
(Introducing Jackie on his
first Ed Sullivan show appearance)

"Jackie Wilson was one of the greatest entertainers that I ever worked with, and I did quite a few shows with him. And he was very, very creative. The things that you see James Brown [do], the people who do that [kind of] entertaining that are dancing and what have you, Jackie and Joe Tex are the ones who originated that kind of stuff. But, ah, Jackie, Jackie Wilson was a very good entertainer and I don't know what he would be doing today. Probably right on top because he could entertain and sing. Yeah, I really hated when we lost him because he had so many things going on before he passed."

Bobby "Blue" Bland

"Jackie and I was really great friends. I had been knowing Jackie for years and years. I learned a lot from Jackie Wilson because Jackie Wilson was one of my favorite singers . . . The first time I met him was when we were on the same package show in Atlanta at The Royal Peacock on Auburn Avenue. So it was pretty exciting. I got all his records, you know. We really miss him. Matter of fact, on my next LP we're doing in Hollywood I'm going to be doing a song dedicated to Jackie."

Percy Sledge

"I admired Jackie Wilson, and I idolized Jackie Wilson.... Well, Jackie Wilson says he idolized me too, because when I hit the stage, Jackie, whoever, Sam Cooke, they used to come on the stage with me 'cause I was getting all the glory. . . . Jackie used to always come on stage with me. Jackie was dangerous. I was scared when he come on stage, 'cause Jackie was... I mean he was one of the badest entertainers I ever saw on stage.

Odell "Gorgeous" George

"We were on this high stage there in Jacksonville, just singing, and all of a sudden I felt somebody pulling me face down on the stage and then he hit that high note and the chandelier was falling on the stage. . . . Several nightclubs we used to work, they had to take the glasses off the wall when he sang that tune because the champagne glasses would tumble down and break. That happened at the Step Show Lounge in Philadelphia."

Bill Murry

"Jackie Wilson's solo career with Brunswick Records lasted from 1957 to 1975 during which time he recorded over 350 sides. Yet, inexplicably for a singer considered to be one of *the* voices of black music, the music legacy he has left behind remains largely unexplored outside of the obvious and abundant "hits" compilations... His was truly one of the most sublime voices of all time."

Steve Bryant
(Liner Notes)

"Jackie Wilson, pioneer showman of the old rhythm and blues school, possessed the most acrobatic voice in black music. From sonorous full throated howls of passion to a growl akin to gravel in a food blender, Wilson laced his powerfully expressive singing with polish, panache ,and melismatic decoration on a heart-stopping scale."

Bill Millar
(Liner Notes)

"Though it is hard to document, it is the unfulfilled immensity of Wilson's gifts that make him one of R&B's greatest tragedies. As a live performer only James Brown, another ex-boxer, could match Wilson for sheer athleticism. But where Brown projected the gritty determination of a heavyweight—left hooks and thrusting thighs—Wilson was a devilishly agile middleweight, pound for pound one of the most graceful entertainers ever. Wilson was able to leap from a platform to the stage, land on his toes and knees and then elevate purposefully to his feet without missing a note. Anyone who ever saw him, either live or on television, will never forget the image of Wilson, snazzy sharkskin pants rubbing against the floor, his shirt open to his waist, his processed hair flying about his head, and the crowds roaring with the frenzy of a ritual sacrifice. There was always an air of danger at a Wilson show, since one never knew what the audience or the singer would do next."

Nelson George (in)

<u>The Death of Rhythm and Blues</u>

"One day the history of pop music will be written and when it is this man's name will be at the top, and I guarantee he's one of the greatest entertainers in the world—the fabulous Jackie Wilson."

Jerry Lee Lewis

(Television show introduction-1971)

"...melisma, the vocal art of stretching a word or a syllable up, down and sideways along the scale. This is what lets Aretha Franklin make one word, like "good" into an entire song. These are the vocal aeronautics that let Smokey Robinson's falsetto soar as easily as a hawk on a mountain air draft. Jackie Wilson used it so well he could get nearly two dozen notes out of a single word."

Gerri Hersey (in)

<u>Nowhere to Run: The Story of Soul Music</u>

"My first national tour was with Jackie Wilson and he was like a big brother to me. He taught me all about getting on and off a stage successfully, about an entertainer's 'territory.' He always gave his audiences pure excitement, and I believe Jackie was a major influence for all music. He was the innovator . . . with the dance, movements and energy you see now with Michael Jackson, Prince and others. We all miss him but when I think of Jackie, I know we are all better for having had him as a part of our industry."

Dionne Warwick

(Rhino liner notes)

"Wilson was the ultimate victim of the exploitative nature of the record business. His victimization became dreadfully manifest in his final years in the image that most fans retain of the singer, that of a bedridden, brain-damaged, almost vegetative man who for eight years was shunted from nursing home to nursing home like an embarrassment, while his ex-wives fought between themselves and with his record company and the IRS over his fast-depleting estate.

"Had Wilson been a minor R&B talent scarcely anyone would have noticed his plight. Yet he was one of the greats, whose tragedy was compounded by the fact he had never received his due during the course of his career not only in the rhythm 'n blues field but also as one of the great early rock 'n roll stars. The one big question observers ask is how could this enormously talented entertainer... not achieve the heights of success of a Sam Cooke or a James Brown?"

Robert Pruter

"That was Jackie Wilson, one of the most trusting souls I've ever known. Maybe that seemingly blind faith is what caused him to be involved with some of the questionable people he chose to have around him. Maybe that trust is part of what made him one of the most daring and courageous performers of his time."

Billy Vera
(Rhino album cover)

"Boston's Back Bay Theater was jammed to capacity, filled with a noisy, enthusiastic throng, out to see the latest of the traveling soul revues. This show promised to be something special, with a rare visit from Roy Hamilton, the urbane crooner of *Ebb Tide*, and an appearance by Jackie Wilson, the man responsible for *Lonely Teardrops* and *That's Why*. But as the warmup acts went through their paces, all was not well backstage; the show's promoter was on the phone jabbering frantically to Roy Hamilton's agent, who had no idea where his singer was. It soon became clear that Hamilton wouldn't show.

"Fearful of the wrath of the fevered crowd if one of the headliners failed to appear, the promoter urgently whispered in Jackie Wilson's ear as he prepared to go on; Wilson, after a moment's pause, agreed. Bounding on-stage, he grabbed the mike, spun around and raced into a blistering version of *That's Why (I Love You So)*. For over an hour, Jackie Wilson played to the screaming audience, teasing the women clustered in front of the stage. Suddenly, in the middle of *Shake! Shake! Shake!,* he jumped into a sea of outstretched arms. With the mike in hand, he attempted to sing, but women, clawing ravenously, shredded his shirt. Finally, Wilson's body disappeared. The theater was in turmoil; the audience pressed forward, hoping to catch a glimpse of what was going on. After minutes of pushing and shoving, the police escorted Wilson to safety. The lights were turned on and everybody ordered out. No one missed Roy Hamilton."

Joe McEwen & Gregg Geller
The Jackie Wilson Story
(Album liner notes)

"I find certain people will not clap for certain songs but they will clap for the songs they came to hear. . . . Some people want to cry, some come to laugh, some come for the knock-down-drag-out, some come to plain listen, study. Some come because they just enjoy watching their favorite performer. It's a beautiful feeling and a beautiful thing to see."

Jackie Wilson

There is no bigger word in the English language than "if." If Jackie had taken the high road, if he had paced himself, if he had within him the common sense or business sense to take an active role in decision-making regarding his own career, if he hadn't been driven into an early grave—he might still be performing today like his good friend Chuck Jackson.

Two cliches describe Jackie and Chuck Jackson's relationship— two peas in a pod, and partners in crime. They gambled together and went off on women chasing binges. Lamar Cochran, who once chauffeured for Jackson as well as Jackie, said about the two men, "They could communicate 'cause they was like cock hounds together. Both of them. This was their thing." In fact, Chuck idolized Jackie because underneath all the exterior arrogance people sometimes ascribed to Jackie, he never failed to help a friend in need. After a long string of near misses with the Del-Vikings and solo records on a variety of labels, Jackie gave Chuck a spot in a Jackie Wilson Revue at the Apollo Theater. It would prove to be Chuck's big break, for in the audience during one of those shows were Luther Dixon and Florence Greenberg, the brains behind Scepter Records.

From the jacket liner of *Chuck Jackson—The Great Recordings* compact disc set on the Rhino Records Tomato label, Jackson picked up the story in an interview with Diana Reid Haig: "Jackie was giving me a great feature in the show when we hit the Apollo. Two or three days into our run there, several companies came to me and wanted me to record for them, including Brunswick, Columbia, and RCA. One day this white woman and this black man came to my dressing room and told me how much they loved my shows and my voice. They said, 'We have a record company, and we have the Shirelles. We're small and we don't have much front money to give you, but we really believe in you. If you come with us, we'll make you a star.'"

"Out of all the companies that spoke to me, Florence and Luther were the only people that I thought were sincere. So I prayed about it. I said, 'Lord, I hope I'm doing the right thing turning down all these major labels, but I'm going with Scepter.' And that decision was the best thing that ever happened to me."

Jackson went on to chart twenty recordings on *Billboard's* R&B and pop charts between 1961 and 1967, with three of them reaching the R&B Top Ten, all with Scepter. Because Scepter was not a slavemaster, Jackson broke with them after many years to try something new. He spent some time trying to mold himself into the Motown sound, which directly opposed the kind of music he had been recording in New York, and found the fit was not good. Nonetheless, Jackson continued to perform through the 1980s and 1990s at a solid pace with a large following of fans who relish original New York style soul.

Or, Jackie may have blazed the comeback trail, riding the Retro revival like his close friend LaVern Baker, an Apollo Theater veteran with twenty rhythm and blues hits during the ten-year period between 1955 and 1965. Like Jackie she suffered a slight career cooling off period during the late sixties, but she made the most of her talent by traveling to Vietnam to entertain troops and then managing a club near a military base in the Philippines for twenty years. Baker died in March 1997 but not before enjoying a strong career resurgence in 1990 in the Broadway production of *Black and Blue*. She had also released an album of her nightclub acts in 1992.

According to Gorgeous George, Jackie was already on the road to making a comeback. "Jackie Wilson was a star, believe me. He was a star until the end. And matter of fact, when he was going to Atlantic City, his last show when he had a stroke, he was making a comeback, a big comeback."

Chuck Barry, James Brown, Jimi Hendrix, Stevie Wonder, Ray Charles, Diana Ross, Whitney Houston, and Michael Jackson—all of them were prodigious talents that transcended the boundaries of race. So, it is not enough to claim that Jackie did not achieve the status of the white Elvis simply because his skin was black. It is certainly untrue that Elvis had a better singing voice than Jackie and Elvis would be the first to admit it. He once said, "My voice is ordinary; if I stand still while I'm singing, I'm a dead man."

It falls short of an explanation to allege Jackie's drug and alcohol abuse kept him from achieving the acclaim he deserved because history has proven this is not a hindrance in the world of rock 'n roll. Nor is it enough to claim that he failed to achieve the status and popularity of the white Elvis because he refused to bend to the recommendations and guidance of his management or, depending on whom you believe, because he resisted change himself. In defense of Nat Tarnopol, perhaps he was just not up to the challenge of managing someone as vivid and exceptional as Jackie. Where Jackie may have been destined for Hollywood, Nat could only see as far as the next nightclub or armory booking. Nat had control of Jackie's career but he may not have been able to later take control of his personal life, provide competent direction or a shoulder to lean on in times of need, when the crises of Jackie's life occurred. Although the Circuit Court of Appeals judge who over-turned his convictions called Brunswick's contract with Jackie "ruth-less," Nat may only have been guilty of being too weak. (After 1981 Brunswick ceased to exist except to reissue masters to other labels. Tarnopol moved to Las Vegas sometime around 1985 and died of a heart attack on Christmas day, 1987.)

In comparing the successes of Elvis and Jackie Wilson, one can-not overlook the influence of the people behind them. Colonel Parker never had any interest above that of Elvis. He negotiated profitable contracts for Elvis's movies, earning him $2.3 million for his first seven film rolls, $250,000 for *Jailhouse Rock.* Parker watched over Elvis's image, carefully sculpting and protecting it as needed. In the movie *Love Me Tender* Elvis is supposed to die in the end. Parker would not have his star killed, even symbolically. The script was rewritten and the ending re-shot. The final version, however, did include an Elvis death scene. Surely the Colonel re-ceived other concessions for giving in.

In his article *Jackie Wilson. Lonely Teardrops and Endless Trag-edy,* Al Duckett cites Bobby Schiffman's opinion regarding whether or not Jackie was exploited by Nat Tarnopol, or whether he was his own worst enemy. Schiffman was the former managing director of the 125th Street Apollo, having succeeded its founder, Frank Schiffman. Keeping in mind Schiffman was friends with both Jackie and Nat Tarnopol: "I love Jackie Wilson," Schiffman says. "But I have to say that, in my honest opinion, Nat Tarnopol was Jackie's best friend and Jackie was his own worst enemy. I know, for a fact, that Nat, rather than exploiting him did his best to protect Jackie's money. I have to say that, in all probability, Jackie created all or most of his own problems. One factor, I believe, had to do with Jackie's inability or unwillingness to change, to adjust to trends and social movements. When the nationalistic flavor in the black community began to turn its back on processed hair, the conkolene, and their attempt to be white, Jackie refused to change. He continued to gas his hair and to cultivate the slick look which had fallen from favor."

Major Robinson, Wilson's former press agent, agrees with Schiffman that many blacks saw this attitude of Wilson's as a "repudiation of the attempt to be progressive and to defy significant social movement." Schiffman and Robinson also concur in the feeling that the success of Wilson's personal appearances deteriorated because Jackie also failed to change his demeanor.

Schiffman concludes: "Jackie was one of the most lovable personalities in the business. He was a superstar in his time and he could have had the longevity as a superstar of an Eckstine or a Sinatra. But he was the personification of the star with all the inherent problems resulting from people standing around, telling him he was the nearest thing to Jesus. It's terribly tragic."

Tragic indeed. Duckett takes the position that Jackie Wilson was a Gemini and had a dual personality. His stage and performing persona were charismatic, everyone loved him, and his fans, especially the women, were wild about him. The stories told by the people closest to him are vastly different. Duckett claims Jackie was arrogant, irresponsible, and dictatorial, that he had many personal and professional problems he brought on himself. "They tell you the humility which he wore in public seemed to be a mask for the kind of cockiness he projected in private."

Duckett writes: "Major Robinson, the savvy New York publicist who helped to embellish the Jackie Wilson image for eight years, knows about Jackie and money. Major recalls one instance when Jackie had played a smash engagement at the Harlem 125th Street Apollo Theater. Quoting Robinson - 'The lines were stretching all the way across 125th Street and around the corner,' Major reminisces. 'The box office take was a record figure—$54,000. One closing night, aware that he owed me several hundred for past services, Jackie asked me to meet him the following day after he had returned to the Apollo to get his money. I knew that his end of the deal was something like $35,000. But when we got together, he took me into a bar down the street and explained that he could only give me half of the money, a couple of hundred. I wasn't worried. He was my man and he always paid me. But I was shocked that he would be short a couple of hundred after generating that kind of income. I got the money later, but I never understood.'"

And neither do we. Did Jackie make any kind of accounting of his income and expenses? Or, was that job the sole discretion of the nice guy mobster, Johnny Roberts?

Duckett further finds it is "ironic" that anyone would compare the earnings of Elvis's verses to those of Jackie Wilson. Although he fails to explain the meaning of the word in context, he goes on to relate a story about the two of them told to him by Robinson. "Once, during a Hollywood engagement starring Wilson, Major recalls, Presley came to the night club every night to sit and watch Jackie for hours. After the show, he would take Jackie and Major on the set with him where Presley was doing a film. One afternoon, Major remembers, Wilson admired a handsome watch Elvis was wearing and commented on it. Presley took the watch off and gave it to him."

Is fame the culprit in the tragedy of Jackie Wilson? Is fame so cruel a master only the emotionally strong survive? Elvis was avidly searching for fame when it stuck a hammer blow in his life in 1957. At the beginning of the year he could walk around Memphis, shop for clothes at Lansky's, grab a hamburger. By the end of the year after a few television performances, hordes of fans were pushing and shoving each other just to touch him. Crowds stampeded like a herd of parched cattle toward water whenever he was spotted in public. Perplexed and frightened by the dramatic shift in people's reaction to him and his music, he surrounded himself with body guards and trusted associates who later became known as the Memphis Mafia. We would try in many ways to make him ours, but we would never get near him again.

There is, however, a fantastic irony about a talented black performer being influenced by a talented white performer who was himself influenced by black performers. The relationship between Jackie Wilson and Elvis Presley is, in fact, a micro-version of the development of 20th century popular music—the yin and the yang of black and white music that resulted in rock *'n* roll as we now know it.

Elvis and Jackie found the fame they craved, yet both were perpetually, horribly alone and sought refuge from that loneliness down any forlorn avenue that would help them elude the nightmarish reality of their lives. Twenty years later we are still mourning their deaths. We have yet to realize or admit that because we wished to possess them, they were filled with *Lonely Teardrops.* Then we checked them into a room at the *Heartbreak Hotel* and promptly swallowed the key.

THE END

Discography 1952-1977

SINGLES	Label	Release
As Sonny Wilson:		
Rainy Day Blues/Rockaway Rock	Dee-Gee	1952
Danny Boy/Bulldozer Blues	Dee-Gee	1952

Billy Ward and the Dominoes (with Wilson as lead vocal):

	Label	Release
Where Now, Little Heart/You Can't Keep a Good Man Down	Federal	07/53
Rags To Riches/Don't Thank Me	King	10/53
Christmas in Heaven/Ringing In A Brand New Year	King	11/53
Until The Real Thing Comes Along/My Baby's 3-D	Federal	12/53
Tootsie Roll/I'm Gonna Move To The Outskirts of Town	Federal	03/54
Tenderly/A Little Lie	King	04/54
Three Coins In A Fountain/Lonesome Road	King	05/54
Little Things Mean A Lot/I Really Don't Want to Know	King	06/54
Come To Me Baby/Gimme Gimme Gimme	Jubilee	09/54
Above Jacob's Ladder/Little Black Train	Federal	10/54
If I Never Get To Heaven/Can't Do Sixty No More	Federal	02/55
Love Me Now Or Let Me Go/Caveman	Federal	04/55
May I Never Love Again/Learnin' The Blues	King	07/55
Sweethearts In Paradise/Take Me Back To Heaven	Jubilee	08/55
Give Me You/Over The Rainbow	King	09/55
Bobby Sox Baby/How Long, How Long Blues	Federal	05/56
St. Therese Of The Roses/		
Home Is Where You Hang Your Heart	Decca	06/56
Will You Remember/Come On Snake Let's Crawl	Decca	08/56
Half A Love/Evermore	Decca	12/56
Rock, Plymouth Rock/'Til Kingdom Come	Decca	01/57
One Moment With You/St. Louis Blues	Federal	07/57

To Each His Own/I Don't Stand A Ghost of A Chance	Decca	09/57
September Song/When The Saints Go Marching In	Decca	11/57
Lay It On The Line/		
That's When You Know You're Growing Old	King	04/61

As Jackie Wilson:

Reet Petite/By the Light of the Silvery Moon	Brunswick	08/57
To Be Loved/Come Back to Me	Brunswick	02/58
As Long As I Live/I'm Wanderin'	Brunswick	05/58
We Have Love/Singing a Song	Brunswick	08/58
Lonely Teardrops/In the Blue of Evening	Brunswick	10/58
That's Why/Love is All	Brunswick	03/59
I'll Be Satisfied/Ask	Brunswick	06/59
You Better Know It/Never Go Away	Brunswick	08/59
Talk That Talk/Only You, Only Me	Brunswick	10/59
Night/Doggin' Around	Brunswick	03/60
All My Love/A Woman, A Lover, A Friend	Brunswick	06/60
Alone At Last/Am I the Man	Brunswick	09/60
My Empty Arms/Tear of the Year	Brunswick	12/60
Please Tell Me Why/Your One and Only Love	Brunswick	02/61
I'm Coming on Back to You/Lonely Life	Brunswick	05/61
Years From Now/You Don't Know What it Means	Brunswick	07/61
The Way I Am/My Heart Belongs to Only You	Brunswick	10/61
The Greatest Hurt/There'll Be No Next Time	Brunswick	12/62
I Found Love/There's Nothing Like Love (w/ Linda Hopkins)	Brunswick	03/62
Hearts/Sing	Brunswick	04/62
I Just Can't Help It/ My Tale of Woe	Brunswick	06/62
Forever and a Day/Baby That's All	Brunswick	09/62
What Good Am I Without You/A Girl Named Tamiko	Brunswick	12/62
Baby Workout/I'm Going Crazy	Brunswick	02/63
Shake A Hand/Say I Do (w/ Linda Hopkins)	Brunswick	05/63
Shake, Shake, Shake/He's a Fool	Brunswick	06/63
Baby Get It/The New Breed	Brunswick	09/63
O Holy Night/Silent Night	Brunswick	11/63
I'm Travelin' On/Haunted House	Brunswick	02/64
Call Her Up/The Kickapoo	Brunswick	03/64
Big Boss Line/Be My Girl	Brunswick	05/64

Squeeze Her, Tease Her/Give Me Back My Heart	Brunswick	08/64
She's All Right/Watch Out	Brunswick	09/64
Danny Boy/Soul Time	Brunswick	02/65
When The Saints Go Marching In/		
Yes Indeed (w/ Linda Hopkins)	Brunswick	04/65
No Pity in the Naked City/I'm So Lonely	Brunswick	06/65
I Believe I'll Love You/Lonely Teardrops	Brunswick	10/65
Think Twice/Please Don't Hurt Me (w/ LaVern Baker)	Brunswick	12/65
I've Got To Get Back/3 Days, 1 Hour, 30 Minutes	Brunswick	01/66
Brand New Thing/Soul Galore	Brunswick	03/66
Be My Love/I Believe	Brunswick	05/66
Whispers/The Fairest of Them All	Brunswick	09/66
I Don't Want to Lose You/Just Be Sincere	Brunswick	01/67
I've Lost You/Those Heartaches	Brunswick	04/67
Higher and Higher/I'm the One To Do It	Brunswick	07/67
Since You Showed Me How to Be Happy/The Who Who Song	Brunswick	11/67
For Your Precious Love/Uptight (w/ Count Basie)	Brunswick	01/68
Chain Gang/Funky Broadway (w/ Count Basie)	Brunswick	04/68
I Get the Sweetest Feeling/Nothing But Blue Skies	Brunswick	06/68
For Once In My Life/You Brought About a Change	Brunswick	10/68
I Still Love You/Hum De Dum De Do	Brunswick	02/69
Helpless/Do It The Right Way	Brunswick	08/69
Do Your Thing/With These Hands	Brunswick	11/69
Let This Be a Letter to My Baby/Didn't I	Brunswick	04/70
This Love Is Real/Love Uprising	Brunswick	11/70
Say You Will/This Guy's In Love With You	Brunswick	04/71
Love Is Funny That Way/Try It Again	Brunswick	10/71
You Got Me Walking/The Fountain	Brunswick	01/72
The Girl Turned Me On/Forever and a Day	Brunswick	04/72
You Left The Fire Burning/What a Lovely Way	Brunswick	07/72
Beautiful Day/What'cha Gonna Do About Love	Brunswick	01/73
Because of You/Go Away	Brunswick	04/73
No More Goodbyes/Sing a Little Song	Brunswick	07/73
It's All Over/Shake a Leg	Brunswick	11/73
Don't Burn No Bridges/Don't Burn No Bridges (Instr.)	Brunswick	10/75
Nobody But You/I've Learned About Life	Brunswick	1977

EXTENDED PLAY RECORDINGS

The Versatile Jackie Wilson	Brunswick	05/58
Jumpin' Jack	Brunswick	12/58
That's Why	Brunswick	04/59
Talk That Talk	Brunswick	05/60
Mr. Excitement	Brunswick	07/60
Jackie Wilson	Brunswick	11/60
So Much	Brunswick	03/61
The Greatest Hurt	Brunswick	12/61
I Just Can't Help It	Brunswick	06/62
Baby Workout	Brunswick	02/63
Shake a Hand (with Linda Hopkins)	Brunswick	05/63

ALBUMS:

Billy Ward and the Dominoes:

Billy Ward and the Dominoes	Decca	01/57
Billy Ward and the Dominoes	King	04/61

Jackie Wilson:

He's So Fine	Brunswick	03/58
Lonely Teardrops	Brunswick	02/59
So Much	Brunswick	11/59
Jackie Sings the Blues	Brunswick	04/60
My Golden Favorites	Brunswick	08/60
A Woman, A Lover, A Friend	Brunswick	11/60
You Ain't Heard Nothin' Yet	Brunswick	02/61
Jackie Wilson By Special Request	Brunswick	09/61
Body & Soul	Brunswick	04/62
Jackie Wilson At the Copa	Brunswick	08/62
Jackie Wilson Sings the World's Greatest Melodies	Brunswick	01/63
Baby Work Out	Brunswick	04/63
Shake a Hand (w/ Linda Hopkins)	Brunswick	07/63
Merry Christmas from Jackie Wilson	Brunswick	10/63
My Golden Favorites, Vol. 2	Brunswick	11/63
Somethin' Else	Brunswick	06/64
Soul Time	Brunswick	04/65
Spotlight on Jackie Wilson	Brunswick	09/65
Soul Galore	Brunswick	02/66

Whispers	Brunswick	12/66
Higher and Higher	Brunswick	10/67
Manufacturers of Soul (w/ Count Basie)	Brunswick	03/68
I Get the Sweetest Feeling	Brunswick	10/68
Jackie Wilson's Greatest Hits	Brunswick	03/69
Do Your Thing	Brunswick	10/69
It's All a Part of Love	Brunswick	02/70
This Love Is Real	Brunswick	03/70
You Got Me Walking	Brunswick	11/71
Jackie Wilson's Greatest Hits	Brunswick	10/72
Beautiful Day	Brunswick	03/73
Nowstalgia	Brunswick	1974
Nobody But You	Brunswick	1975

Select Bibliography

Books

Brown, James. **James Brown- The Godfather of Soul** (New York: Thunder's Mouth Press).

Brown,Ruth with Yule, Donald. **Miss Rhythm: The Autobiolgraphy of Ruth Brown, Rhythm & Blues Legend** (New York: Donald I. Fine Books).

Cavendish, Marshal. **The Marshall Cavendish Illustrated History of Popular Music**, Volume I (New York).

Clark, Dick; Robinson, Richard. **Rock and Roll Remembers** (New York: Thomas Y. Crowell Company, 1976).

Clark, Dick, Ed. **Best of American Bandstand: Superstars**

Clark, Dick with Bronson, Fred. **Dick Clark's American Bandstand**, (Collins Publishers, 1997).

Clark, Donald, Ed. **The Penguin Encyclopedia of Popular Music**, (New York: Penguin Books, 1990).

Cotton, Lee. **Reelin' & Rockin' Volume 11:**1956-1959 (U.S.: Popular Culture, Inc.1995).

Cotton, Lee. **Shake, Rattle & Roll- The Golden Age of American Rock & Roll, Volume I 1952-1955** (Popular Culture, Inc., 1989)

Dannen, Fredric. **Hit Men** (New York: First Vintage Books, 1991).

Eliot, Marc. **The Money Behind the Music** (New York: Franklin Watts, 1989).

Esposito, Joe; Oumano, Elena. **Good Rockin' Tonight** (New York: Avon Books, 1994).

Fox, Ted. **Showtime At The Apollo** (New York: Da Capo Press, 1993).

Fox, Ted. **In the Groove: The People Behind the Music** (New York: St. Martin's Press, 1986).

George, Nelson. **The Death of Rhythm & Blues** (New York: Pantheon Books).

Gordy, Jr., Berry. **To Be Loved** (New York: Warner Books, 1994).

Gregory, Hugh. **Soul Music A-Z.** Revised edition (New York: Da Capo Press, 1995).

Herman, Gary. **Rock 'n' Roll Babylon** (New York: Perigee Books,

1982).

Hildebrand, Lee. **Stars of Soul and Rhythm & Blues** (New York: Billboard Books, 1994).

Hirshey, Gerri. **Nowhere To Run, The Story of Soul Music** (New York: Da Capo Press, 1994).

Jackson, John A. **Big Beat Heat** (New York: Schirmer Books, Macmillan,1991).

James, Etta: Ritz, David. **Rage to Survive** (New York: Villard Books, 1995).

LaBelle, Patty with Randolph, Laura B. *Don't Block the Blessing: Revelations of a Lifetime* (New York: Riverhead Books, 1996).

Marsh, Dave. **The First Rock & Roll Confidential Report** (New York: Pantheon, 1985).

Millar, Bill. **The Drifters: The Rise and Fall of the Black Vocal Group** (New York: The Macmillan Company).

Nash, Allana. **Elvis Aaron Presley- Revelations from the Memphis Mafia** (New York: Harper Collins, 1995).

Pierce, Patricia Jobe. **The Ultimate Elvis** (New York: Simon and Schuster).

Pruter, Robert. **Chicago Soul** (University of Illinois Press, 1982).

Rees, Dafydd; Crampton, Luke. **Rock Movers & Shakers** (New York: Billboard Books, 1991).

Robinson, Smokey with Ritz, David. **Inside My Life** (New York: McGraw Hill, 1988).

Sandahl, Linda. **Rock Films** (New York: Facts on File Publications, 1987).

Shaw, Arnold. **The World of Soul- Black America's Contribution to The Pop Music Scene** (New York: Cowles, 1970).

Shaw, Arnold. **Black Popular Music in America** (New York: Macmillan Collier, 1986).

Shaw, Arnold. **Honkers and Shouters: The Golden Years of Rhythm & Blues** (New York: Macmillan,19780.

Singleton, Raynoma Gordy; Brown, Bryan;Eichler, Mim. **Berry, Me and Motown** (Chicago: Contemporary Books, 1990).

Stallings, Penny. **Rock 'n'Roll Confidential** (Boston: Little, Brown. and Company, 1984).

Stanley, David E.;Coffey, Frank. **The Elvis Encyclopedia** (Santa Monica: General Publishing Group, Inc., 1994).

West, Red, West, Sonny; Hebler, Dave; Dunleavy, Steve. **Elvis: What Happened?** (New York: Ballentine Books, 1977).

Wolff, Daniel. **You Send Me: The Life and Times of Sam Cooke** (New York: William Morrow and Company, 1995).

Worth, Fred; Tamerius, Steve D. **Elvis- His Life from A to Z** (New Jersey: Wings Books, 1992).

Supporting Research
Reference

American Rock 'n' Roll Tour by Dave Walker (New York: Thunder's Mountain Press, 1992).

Encyclopia of Rock & Roll
The End of Something
Elvis Day-By-Day
Illustrated History of Popular Music,

Articles and News Accounts

"Chatter," **People** (July 4, 1977).

Ciabattari, Jane. "Where There's a Will, There's Way for Fans to Sneak a Peek," **Parade** (August 3, 1997).

Corliss, Richard. "From Hound Dog To Lounge Act," **Time** (August 4, 1997).

Duckett, Al. "Jackie Wilson Is No Junkie," **Sepia** (April, 1979).

Duckett, Al. "JackieWilson: Lonely Teardrops and Endless Tragedy," **Sepia**.

Gywnne, S.C. "Love Me Legal Tender," **Time** (August 4, 1997).

Holland, Bill. "Vaults Suffer From Past Pilferages," **Billboard** (July 19, 1997).

"Houston Fans No LIke When Jackie No Show**," New York Amsterdam News** (December 18,1965).

"Jackie Hits Bigtime At Copacabana Open," **New York Amsterdam News** (April 28, 1962).

"Jackie Wilson Mourned by 1,500 During Funeral at Baptist Church in Detroit," **Jet** (February 13, 1984).

"Jackie Wilson, Rock Singer; Records Included "Teardrops" (Obituary), **New York Times** (January 23, 1984).

"Jackie Wilson, Wife Divorcing," **New York Amsterdam News** (March 22, 1969).

Jacobs, Dick; Holmes, Tim. "Jackie Wilson: Taking It Higher: A Producer Remembers Mr. Excitement," **Musician** (October, 1987).

Newman, Ralph M.; Kaltman, Alan. "Lonely Teardrops: The Story of a Forgotten Man," **Time Barrier Express**, # 24 (April-May, 1979).

Pollack, Bill. "Jackie Wilson's Lonely Tears," **Village Voice** (August 14, 1978).

Pruter, Robert. "Jackie Wilson: The Most Tragic Figure in Rhythm "N" Blues," **Goldmine** (November 1, 1991)(.

"Rhythm and Blues LaVern Baker Dies," **The Florida Times-Union**,

(March 12, 1997).

Richardson, Clive. "Hot Gospel" **(Ilustrated History of Popular Music).**

Robinson, Major. "Rock 'n' Roll Idol Jackie Wilson Felled BY Fan's Gun," **Jet** (March 2, 1961).

"Rock 'n' Roll Singer Shot Resisting Fan," **New York Times** (February 16, 1961).

Settle, Ken. "Jackie Wilson: A Celebration of Dignity," **Goldmine** (July 17, 1987).

"Walter Scott's Personality Parade Q & A," **Parade** (April 21, 1996).

Wilson, Mrs. Jackie as told to Robinson, Major. "It's Tough To Be The Wife Of A Star," **Jet** (1961).

Interviews*

Bland, Bobby "Blue"

Campbell, Reverend Dr. Anthony

Cameron, G.C.

Cochran, Lamar

Frazier, Bill and Johnson, Richard

George, Odell "Gorgeous"

Guidry, Lynn

Murry, Bill

Redding, Joseph

Sledge, Percy

Washington, Toni Lynn

Wilson, Jackie (interviewed by Norman Knight)

*** All conducted by the author unless otherwise noted**

Album Covers and Liner Notes

Bryant, Steve. CD liner notes, *Jackie Wilson: The Chicago Years, Volume 1,* (Charly Soul, CPCD 8052)1995.

Byrant, Steve. CD liner notes, *The Jackie Wilson Story: The New York Years, Volume 1,* (Charly Soul, JWCD 1)1995.

Byrant, Steve. CD liner notes, *The Jackie Wilson Story: The Chicago Years, Volume 2,* (Charly Soul, JWCD 6)1995.

Byrant, Steve. CD liner notes. *The Jackie Wilson Story: The New York Years, Volume 2,* (Charly Soul, JWCD 2)1995.

Jackie Wilson Hit Story Volume 2, Album liner notes, (Global Arts Productions, Portugal, 1993).

Jackson, Chuck, CD liner notes, *Chuck Jackson: The Great Recordings,* (Tomato label for Rhino Records, 1994).

McEwen, Joel. Album liner notes, *The Jackie Wilson Story,* (CBS, Inc., 1983) Revised and updated version from **McEwen's The**

Rolling Stone Illustrated History of Rock and Roll (Rolling Stone Press, 1980).

Millar, Bill. Album liner notes, *Reet Petite,* (Ace)1984.

Sullivan, Ed. Album liner notes, *Jackie Wilson at the* Copa, (Brunswick BL 54108).

Vera, Billy. Album liner notes, *Jackie Wilson Through the Years,* (Rhino Records, Inc., 1987).

Wilson, Jackie. Album liner notes. *You Ain't Heard Nothin' Yet,* (Brunswick BL 54100).

Index

About the Author

Gale Allen Ellsworth, born September 6, 1946, in Muskogee, Oklahoma, moved to Jacksonville, Florida, in 1956, where he saw Elvis Presley perform live for the first time in August of that year. Interestingly, the year 1956 was also the year Elvis saw Jackie Wilson perform live for the first time.

The author graduated from Englewood High School in 1964 and studied broadcast management in college. Using the name Sandy Shores, he was hired for his first position as a radio personality at WQIK by Marshall Rowland, who hired Elvis for his first Jacksonville appearance on May 13, 1955. In 1970, Ellsworth moved to rival station WVOJ, which changed his radio name to Doug Carter.

In 1973 he moved to Daytona Beach, Florida, and became that city's #1 mid-day announcer for two and one-half years at WMFJ. Other markets included Atlanta, Georgia, Houston, Texas, and Washington, DC.

Ellsworth's writing credits include articles on rhythm and blues pioneers, which are also listed under the name Doug Carter.

On March 17, 1998, at 10:05 a.m., radio personality/author Doug Carter intentionally topped Alan Freed's stunt (as depicted on page 67) by playing Jackie Wilson's song titled *I'll Be Satisfied* for 55 minutes straight on radio station WVOJ in Jacksonville, Florida.